THE ROYAL HOUSE OF NIROLI

Always passionate, always proud.

**The richest royal family in the world—
united by blood and passion, torn apart
by deceit and desire.**

Nestled in the azure blue of the Mediterranean,
the majestic island of Niroli has prospered for
centuries. The Fierezza men have worn the crown
with passion and pride since ancient times.
But now, as the king's health declines,
and his two sons have been tragically killed,
the crown is in jeopardy.

The clock is ticking—a new heir must be found
before the king is forced to abdicate. By royal
decree, the internationally scattered members
of the Fierezza family are summoned to claim
their destiny. But any person who takes
the throne must do so according to
"The Rules of the Royal House of Niroli."
Soon secrets and rivalries emerge as the
descendants of this ancient royal line vie for
position and power. Only a true Fierezza can
become ruler—a person dedicated to their
country, their people...and their eternal love!

The Official Fierezza Family Tree

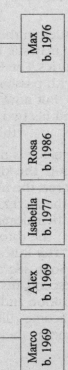

Penny Jordan

THE FUTURE KING'S
PREGNANT MISTRESS

Always passionate, always proud.

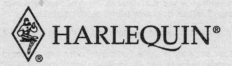

TORONTO • NEW YORK • LONDON
AMSTERDAM • PARIS • SYDNEY • HAMBURG
STOCKHOLM • ATHENS • TOKYO • MILAN • MADRID
PRAGUE • WARSAW • BUDAPEST • AUCKLAND

ISBN-13: 978-0-373-12643-9
ISBN-10:   0-373-12643-3

THE FUTURE KING'S PREGNANT MISTRESS

First North American Publication 2007.

Special thanks and acknowledgment are given to Penny Jordan
for her contribution to *The Royal House of Niroli* series.

The Rules

Rule 1: The ruler must be a moral leader. Any act that brings the Royal House into disrepute will rule a contender out of the succession to the throne.

Rule 2: No member of the Royal House may be joined in marriage without consent of the ruler. Any such union concluded results in exclusion and deprivation of honors and privileges.

Rule 3: No marriage is permitted if the interests of Niroli become compromised through the union.

Rule 4: It is not permitted for the ruler of Niroli to marry a person who has previously been divorced.

Rule 5: Marriage between members of the Royal House who are blood relations is forbidden.

Rule 6: The ruler directs the education of all members of the Royal House, even when the general care of the children belongs to their parents.

Rule 7: Without the approval or consent of the ruler, no member of the Royal House can make debts over the possibility of payment.

Rule 8: No member of the Royal House can accept inheritance nor any donation without the consent and approval of the ruler.

Rule 9: The ruler of Niroli must dedicate their life to the Kingdom. Therefore they are not permitted to have a profession.

Rule 10: Members of the Royal House must reside in Niroli or in a country approved by the ruler. However, the ruler *must* reside in Niroli.

THE ROYAL HOUSE OF NIROLI
Always passionate, always proud.

Each month, Harlequin Presents is delighted
to bring you an exciting installment from
THE ROYAL HOUSE OF NIROLI, in which you can
follow the epic search for the true Nirolian king.
Eight heirs, eight romances, eight fantastic stories!

CHAPTER ONE

MARCO opened his eyes, and looked at the bedside clock: three o'clock in the morning. He'd been dreaming about Niroli—and his grandfather, the king. His heart was still drumming insistently inside his chest, its beat driven by the adrenalin surges of challenge and excitement that reliving one of his past youthful arguments with his grandfather had brought him.

It had been in the aftermath of one of those arguments that Marco had made his decision to prove to himself, and to his grandfather, that he was capable of achieving success somewhere other than Niroli and without his grandfather's influence and patronage. He had been twenty-two then. Now he was thirty-six, and he and his grandfather had long since made a peace—of a sort—even if the older man had never really understood his grandson's refusal to change his mind about his vow to make his own way in the world. Marco had been determined that his success would come *not* as the grandson of the King of Niroli but via his own hard work. As simple Marco Fierezza, a young European entrepreneur, he had used his shrewd grasp of finance to become one of the City of London's most lauded financiers and a billionaire.

In the last few years it had caused Marco a certain amount

of wry amusement to note how his grandfather had turned to him for financial advice with regard to his own private wealth, whilst claiming that their blood tie absolved him of paying for Marco's services! The truth was, his grandfather was a wily old fox who wasn't above using whatever means he could to coerce others into doing what he wanted, often claiming that what he did was done for the good of Niroli, rather than himself.

Niroli!

Outside, the icy cold rain of London rattled against the windows of his Eaton Square apartment, and Marco felt a sudden sharp pang of longing for the beautiful Mediterranean island his family had ruled for so many generations: a sun-drenched jewel of green and gold in an aquamarine sea, from where dark volcanic mountains rose up wreathed in silvery clouds.

The same sea that had claimed the lives of his parents, he reminded himself sombrely, and which had not just robbed him of them, but also made him heir to the throne.

He had always known that ultimately he would become Niroli's king, but he had also believed that this event lay many years away in the future, something he could safely ignore in favour of enjoying his self-created, self-ruled present. However, the reality was that what he had thought of as his distant duty was now about to become his life.

Was that knowledge the reason for the dream he'd had? After all, when it came to the relationship he would have with his grandfather if he agreed to do as King Giorgio had requested and return to Niroli to become its ruler, wasn't there going to be an element of the prodigal male lion at the height of his powers returning to spar with the ageing pack leader? Marco knew and understood the older man very well. His grandfather might claim that he was ready to hand over the royal reins, but Marco suspected that Giorgio would still want to control whoever was holding them as much as he could. And yet, despite his awareness of this, Marco knew that the challenge of ruling Niroli and making it the country he wanted to see it become—by sweeping away the outdated and over-authoritarian structures his grandfather had put in place during his long reign—was one that excited him.

There had never been any doubt in Marco's mind that when ultimately he came to the throne he would make changes to the government of the island that would bring it into the twenty-first century. But then he had also envisaged succeeding his gentle, mild-mannered father, rather than having his tyrannical grandfather standing at his shoulder.

Marco gave a small dismissive shrug. Unlike his late father, a scholarly, quiet man who, Marco had recognised early in his life, had been bullied unmercifully and held in contempt by the King, Marco had never allowed himself to be over-whelmed by his grandfather, even as a child. They shared a common streak of almost brutally arrogant self-belief, and it had been this that had led to the conflict between them. Now, as a mature and powerful man, there was no way Marco intended to allow *anyone* to question his right to do things his own way. That said, he knew that taking the throne would ne-cessitate certain changes in his own lifestyle; there were certain royal rules he would have to obey, if only to pay lip-service to them.

One of those rules forbade the King of Niroli to marry a divorcée. Marco was in no hurry to wed, but when he did he knew he would be expected to make a suitable dynastic union with some pre-approved royal princess of unimpeachable virtue. Somehow he didn't think that it would go down well with his subjects, or the paparazzi, if he were to be seen openly enjoying the company of a mistress, instead of duti-fully finding himself a suitable consort.

He looked towards the bed where Emily lay sleeping, oblivious to what lay ahead and the fast-approaching end of their relationship. Her long blonde hair—naturally blonde, as he had good reason to know—was spread against the pillow. To Marco's surprise, he was suddenly tempted to reach out and twine his fingers through its silken strands, knowing that his touch would wake her, and knowing too that his body was hardening with his immediate need for the intimacy of her body. That he should still desire her so fiercely and so constantly after the length of time they had been together—so very much longer than he'd spent with any woman before—astonished him. But the needs and sexual desires of Marco Fierezza could not be compared with the challenge of becoming the King of Niroli, he acknowledged with his customary arrogance.

King of Niroli.

Emily knew nothing about his connection with Niroli, or his past, and consequently she knew nothing either about his future. Why should she? What reason would there have been for him to tell her, when he had deliberately chosen to live anonymously? He had left Niroli swearing to prove to his grandfather that he could stand on his own feet and make a success of his life without using his royal position, and had quickly discovered that his new anonymity had certain personal advantages; as second in line to Niroli's throne he had grown used to a certain type of predatory woman trying to lure him. His grandfather had warned him when he had been a teenager that he would have to be on his guard, and that he must accept he would never know whether the women who strived to share his bed wanted him for himself, or for who he was. Living in London as Marco Fierezza, rather than Prince Marco of Niroli though he was cynically aware that his combination of wealth and good looks drew the opposite sex to him, he did not attract the kind of feeding frenzy he would have done if he'd been using his royal title. Marco had no objection to rewarding his chosen lovers generously with expensive gifts and a luxurious lifestyle whilst he and they were together. He started to frown. It still irked him that Emily had always so steadfastly—and in his opinion foolishly—refused to accept the presents of jewellery he'd regularly tried to give her.

He'd told her dismissively to think of it as a bonus when she had demanded blankly, 'What's this for?' after he had given her a diamond bracelet to celebrate their first month together.

Her face had gone pale and she'd looked down at the leather box containing the bracelet—a unique piece he'd bought from one of the royal jewellers—her voice as stiff as her body. 'You don't need to bribe me, Marco. I'm with you because I want you, not because I want what you can buy me.'

Now Marco's frown deepened, his reaction to the memory of those words exactly as it had been when Emily had first uttered them. He could feel the same fierce, angry clenching of his muscles and surge of astounded disbelief that the woman who was enjoying the pleasure of his lovemaking and his wealth could dare to suggest that he might need to bribe her to share his bed!

He had soon put Emily in her place though, he reminded himself; his response to her had been a men-acingly silky soft, 'No, you've misunderstood. After all, I already know exactly why you are in my bed and just how much you want me. The bribe, if you wish to think of it as that, is not to keep you there, but to ensure that you leave my bed speedily and silently when I've had enough of having you there.'

She hadn't said anything in reply, but he had seen in her expression what she was feeling. Although he'd never been able to get her to admit to it, he was reasonably sure that her subsequent very convenient business trip, which had taken her away from him for the best part of a week, had been something she had conjured up in an attempt to get back at him. And to make him hungry for her? No woman had the power to make herself so important to him that being with her mattered more than his own iron-clad determination never to allow his emotions to control him and so weaken him. He had grown up seeing how easily his strong-willed grandfather had used his own son's deep love for all those who were close to him to coerce, manipulate and, more often than not in Marco's eyes, humiliate him into doing what King Giorgio wanted. Marco had seen too much to have any illusions about the value of male pride, or the strength of will over gentleness and a desire to please others. Not that Marco hadn't loved his father; he had, so much so that as a young boy he had often furiously resented and verbally attacked his grandfather for the way the older man had treated his immediate heir.

That would never happen to him, Marco had decided then. He would allow no one, not even Niroli's king, to dictate to him.

Marco was well aware that, despite the fact that he had often angered his grandfather with his rebellious ways, the older man held a grudging respect for him. Their pride and their tenacity were attributes they had in common, and in many ways they were alike, although Marco knew that once *he* was Niroli's king there were many changes he would make in order to modernise the kingdom. Marco considered that the way his grandfather ruled Niroli was almost feudal; he'd shared his father's belief that it was essential to give people the opportunity to run their own lives, instead of treating them as his grandfather did, like very young, unschooled children who couldn't be trusted to make their own decisions. He had so many plans for Niroli: it was no wonder he was eager to step out of the role he had created for himself here in London to take on the mantle his birth had fated him to wear! The potential sexual frustration of being without a mistress bothered him a little but, after all, he was a mature man whose ambitions went a lot further than having a willing bed-mate with whom he would never risk making an emotional or legal commitment.

No, he wouldn't let himself miss Emily, he assured himself. The only reason he was giving valuable mental time to thinking about the issue was his concern that she might not accept his announcement that their affair was over as calmly as he wished. He had no desire to hurt her—far from it.

He still hadn't decided just how much he needed to tell her. He would be leaving London, of course, but he suspected that the paparazzi were bound to get wind of what was happening on Niroli, since it was ruled by the wealthiest royal family in the world.

For her own sake, Emily needed to have it made clear to her that nothing they had shared could impinge on his future as Niroli's king. He had never really understood her steadfast refusal to accept his expensive gifts, or to allow him to help her either financially or in any other way with her small interior design business. Because he couldn't understand it, despite the fact that they had been lovers for almost three years, Marco, being the man he was, had inwardly wondered what she might be hoping to gain from him that was worth more to her than his money. It was second nature to him not to trust anyone. Plus, he had learned from observing his grandfather and members of his court what happened to those whose natures allowed others to take advantage of them, as his own father had done.

Marco tensed, automatically shying away from the unwanted pain that thinking about his parents and their deaths could still cause him. He didn't want to acknowledge that pain, and he certainly didn't want to acknowledge the confused feelings he had buried so deeply: pain on his father's behalf, guilt because he could see what his grandfather had been doing to his father and yet he hadn't been able to prevent it, anger with his father for having been so weak, anger with his grandfather for having taken advantage of that weakness, and himself for having seen what he hadn't wanted to see.

He and his grandfather had made their peace, his father was gone, he himself was a man and not a boy any more. It was only in his dreams now that he sometimes revisited the pain of his past. When he did, that pain could be quickly extinguished in the raw passion of satisfying his physical desire for Emily.

But what about the time when Emily would no longer be there? Why was he wasting his time asking himself such foolish questions? Ultimately he would find himself another mistress, no doubt via a discreet liaison with the right kind of woman, perhaps a young wife married to an older husband, though not so young that she didn't understand the rules, of course. He might even, if Emily had been sensible enough, have thought about providing her with the respectability of marriage to some willing courtier in order that they carry on their affair, once he became King of Niroli. But, Marco acknowledged, the very passion that made her such a responsive lover also meant she was not the type who would adapt to the traditional role of royal mistress.

Emily would love Niroli, an island so beautiful and fruitful that ancient lore had said Prometheus himself caused it to rise up from the sea bed so that he could bestow it on mankind.

When Marco thought of the place of his birth, his mental image was one of an island bathed in sunlight, an island so richly gifted by the gods that it was little wonder some legends had referred to it as an earthly paradise.

But where there was great beauty there was also terrible cruelty, as was true of so many legends. The gods had often exacted a terrible price from Niroli for their gifts.

He pushed back the duvet, knowing that he wouldn't be able to sleep now. His body was lean and powerful, magnificently drawn, as though etched by one of the great masters, in the charcoal shadows of the moonlight as he left the bed and padded silently toward the window.

The wind had picked up and was lashing rain against the windows, bending the bare branches of the trees on the street outside. Marco was again transported back to Niroli, where violent storms often swept over the island, whipping up its surrounding seas. The people of Niroli knew not to venture out during the high tides that battered the volcanic rock cliffs of a mountain range so high and so inaccessible in parts that even today it still protected and concealed the bandit descendants of Barbary pirates who long ago had invaded the island. In fact, the fierce seas sucking deep beneath the cliffs had honeycombed them into underwater caves and weakened the rock so that whole sections of it had fallen away. The gales that stirred the seas also tore and ripped at the ancient olive trees and the grapevines on the island, as though to punish them because their harvest had already been plucked to safety.

As a boy Marco had loved to watch the wind savage the land far below the high turrets of the royal castle. He would kneel on the soft padded seating beneath an ancient stone window embrasure, excited by the danger of the storm, wanting to go out and accept the challenge it threw at him. But he had never been allowed to go outside and play as other children did. Instead, at his grandfather's insistence, he'd had to remain within the castle walls, learning about his family's past and his own future role as the island's ultimate ruler.

Inside Marco's head, images he couldn't control were starting to form, curling wraithlike from his childhood memories. It had always been his grandfather and not his parents who had dictated the rules of his childhood, and who'd seen that they were imposed on him...

'Marco, come back to bed. It's cold without you.' Emily's voice was soft and slow, warm, full and sweet with promise, like the fruit of Niroli's vines at the time of harvest, when the grapes lay heavily beneath the sun swollen with ripe readiness and with implicit invitation.

He turned round. He had woken her after all. Emily ran her small interior design business from a small shop-cum-office just off London's Sloane Street. Marco had known from the moment he first saw her at a PR cocktail party that he'd wanted her, and that he'd intended to have her. And he'd made sure that she'd known it too. Marco was used to getting his own way, to claiming his right to direct the course of his own life, even if that meant imposing his will on those who would oppose him. This was an imperative for him, one he refused to be swayed from. He had quickly elucidated that Emily was a divorced woman with no children, and that had made her pattern-card perfect for the role of his mistress. If he had known then her real emotional and sexual history, he knew that he would not have pursued her. But, by the time he had discovered the truth, his physical desire for her had been such that it had been impossible for him to reject her.

He looked towards her now, feeling that desire gripping him again and fighting against it as he had fought all his life against anything or anyone who threatened to control him.

'Marco, something's wrong. What is it?'

Where had it come from, this unwanted ability she seemed to possess of sensing what she could not possibly be able to know? The year his parents died, the storms had come early to Niroli. Marco could remember how when he had first received the news, even before he had said anything, she had somehow guessed that something was wrong. However, whilst she might be intuitive where his feelings were concerned, Emily hadn't yet been shrewd or suspicious enough to make the connection between the announcement of his parents' deaths and the news in the media about the demise of the next in line to the Niroli throne. He remembered how hurt she had looked when he'd informed her that he would be attending his mother and father's funeral without her, but she hadn't said a word. Maybe because she hadn't wanted to provoke a row that might have led to him ending their affair, the reason she didn't want it to end being that, for all her apparent lack of interest in his money, she had to be well aware of what she would lose financially if their relationship came to a close. It was, in Marco's opinion, impossible for any woman to be as unconcerned about the financial benefits of being his mistress as Emily affected to be. It was as his grandfather had warned him: the women who thronged around him expected to be lavishly rewarded with expensive gifts and had no compunction about making that plain.

Under cover of the room's darkness, Emily grimaced to hear the note of pleading in her own voice. Why, when she despised herself so much for what she was becoming, couldn't she stop herself? Was she destined always to have relationships that resulted in her feeling insecure?

'Nothing's wrong,' Marco told her. There was a note in his voice that made her body tense and her emotions flinch despite everything she was trying to do not to let that happen. The trouble was that once you started lying to yourself on an almost hourly, never mind daily, basis about the reality of your relationship, once you started pretending not to notice or care about being the 'lesser' partner, about not being valued or respected enough, you entered a place where the strongest incentive was not to seek out the truth but rather to hide from it. But she had no one but herself to blame for her current situation, she reminded herself.

She had known right from the start what kind of man Marco was, and the type of relationship he wanted with her. The problem was that she had obviously known Marco's agenda rather better than she had understood her own. Although she tried not to do so, sometimes when she was feeling at her lowest—times like now—she couldn't stop herself from giving in to the temptation of fantasising about how Marco could be different: he would not be so fabulously wealthy or arrogantly sexy that he could have any woman he wanted, but instead he'd be just an ordinary man with ordinary goals—a happy marriage, a wife… Her heart kicked heavily, turning over in a slow grind of pain. She thought of children—theirs— and it turned over again, the pain growing more intense.

Why, why, *why* had she been such a fool and fallen in love with Marco? He had made it plain from the start what he wanted from her and what he would give her back in return, and love had never been part of the deal. But then, way back when, she had never imagined that she would fall for him. At the beginning, she had wanted Marco so much, she had been happy to go along with a purely sexual relationship, for as long as he wanted her.

No, she had no one but herself to blame for the constant pain she was now having to endure, the deceit she was having to practise and the fear that haunted her: one day soon Marco would sense that deceit and leave her. She loathed herself so much for her own weakness and for not having the guts to ac- knowledge her love or take the consequences of walking away from him, through the inevitable fiery consuming pain. But, who knew? Maybe walking away from Marco would have a phoenix-like effect on her and allow her to find freedom as a new person. She was such a coward, though, that she couldn't take that step. Hadn't someone once said that a brave man died only once but a coward died a thousand times? So it was for her. She knew that she ought to leave and deal with her feelings, but instead she stayed and suffered a thousand hurtful recognitions every day of Marco's lack of love for her.

But he desired her, and she couldn't bring herself to give up the fragile hope that maybe, just maybe, things would change, and one day he would look at her and know that he loved her, that one day he would allow her to access that part of himself he guarded with such ferocity and tell her that he wanted them to be together for ever...

CHAPTER TWO

THAT was Emily's dream. But the reality was, recently, she'd felt as if they were growing further apart rather than closer. She'd told herself yesterday morning she would face her fear. She took a deep breath.

'Marco, I've always been open and…and honest with you…' It was no good, she couldn't do it. She couldn't make herself ask him that all-important question: 'Do you want to end our relationship?' And, besides, she hadn't always been honest with him, had she? She hadn't told him, for instance, that she had fallen in love with him. Her heart gave another painful lurch.

Marco was watching her, his head inclined towards her. He wore his thick dark hair cut short, but not so short that she couldn't run her fingers through it, shaping the hard bone beneath it as she held him to her when they made love. There was just enough light for her to see the gleam in his eyes, as though he'd guessed the direction her thoughts had taken and knew how much she wanted him. Marco had the most piercingly direct look she'd ever known. He'd focused it on her the night they'd met, when she had tried to cling to reason and rationality, instead of letting herself be blatantly seduced by a pair of tawny-brown predator's eyes…

Emily knew she should make her stand now and demand an explanation for the change she could sense in Marco, but her childhood made it difficult for her to talk openly about her emotions. Instead she hid them away behind locked doors of calm control and self-possession. Was it because she was afraid of what might happen if she allowed her real feelings to get out of control? Because she was afraid of bringing the truth out into the open? Something *was* wrong. Marco *had* changed: he had become withdrawn and preoccupied. There was no way she could pretend otherwise. Had he grown tired of her? Did he want to end their relationship? Wouldn't it be better, wiser, more self-respecting, if she challenged him to tell her the truth? Did she really think that if she ignored her fears they would simply disappear?

'You say that you've always been open and honest with me, Emily, but that isn't the truth, is it?'

Emily's heart somersaulted with slow, sickening despair. He knew? Somehow he had guessed what she was thinking and—almost as bad—she could see he was spoiling for an argument... because that would give him an excuse to end things.

'Remember the night I took you to dinner and you told me about your marriage? Remember how "open" you were with me then—and what you didn't tell me?' Marco recalled sarcastically.

Emily couldn't speak. A mixture of relief and anguish filled her. Her marriage! All this time she had thought—believed—that Marco had understood the scars her past had inflicted on her, but now she realised that she had been wrong. 'It wasn't deliberate, you know that,' she told him, fighting not to let her voice tremble. 'I didn't deliberately hold back anything.' Why was he bringing that up now? she wondered. Surely he wasn't planning to use it as an excuse to get rid of her? He wasn't the kind of man who needed an excuse to do anything, she told herself. He was too arrogant to feel he needed to soften any blows he had to deliver.

Marco looked away from Emily, irritated with himself for saying what he had. Why had he brought up her marriage now, when the last thing he wanted was the danger involved in the sentimentality of looking back to the beginning of their relationship? But it was too late, he *was* already remembering…

He had taken Emily to dinner, setting the scene for how he had hoped the evening would end by telling her coolly how much he wanted to make love to her and how pleased he was that she was a woman of the world, with a marriage behind her and no children to worry about.

'Just out of interest,' he'd quizzed her, 'what was the reason for your divorce?' If there was anything in her past, he wanted to know about it before things went any further.

For a moment he thought that she was going to refuse to answer him. But then her eyes widened slightly and he knew that she had correctly interpreted his question, without him having to spell it out to her. She clearly knew that if she did refuse, their relationship would be over before it had properly begun.

When she finally began to speak, she surprised him with the halting, almost stammering way in which she hesitated and then fiddled nervously with her cutlery, suddenly looking far less calm and in control than he had previously seen her. Her face was shadowed with anxiety and he assumed that the cause of the breakdown in her marriage must have been related to something she had done—such as being unfaithful to her husband. The last thing he expected to hear was what she actually told him. So much so, in fact, that he was tempted to accuse her of lying, but something he saw in her eyes stopped him…

Now Marco shifted his weight from one foot to the other, remembering how shocked he'd been by the unexpected and unwilling compassion he had felt for her as she'd struggled to overcome her reluctance to talk about what was obviously a painful subject...

'I lost my parents in a car accident when I was seven and I was brought up by my widowed paternal grandfather,' she told him.

'He wasn't unkind to me, but he wasn't a man who was comfortable around young children, especially not emotional young girls. He was a retired Cambridge University academic, very gentle and very unworldly. He read the classics to me as bedtime stories. He knew so much about literature but, although I didn't realise it at the time, very little about life. My upbringing with him was very sheltered and protected, very restricted in some ways, especially when I reached my early teens and his health started to deteriorate.

'Gramps' circle of friends was very small, a handful of elderly fellow academics, and...and Victor.'

'Victor?' Marco probed, hearing the hesitation in her voice.

'Yes. Victor Lewisham, my ex-husband. He had been one of Gramps' students, before becoming a university lecturer himself.'

'He must have been considerably older than you?' Marco guessed.

'Twenty years older,' Emily agreed, nodding her head. 'When it became obvious that my grandfather's health was deteriorating, he told me that Victor had agreed to look after me after...in his place. Gramps died a few weeks after that. I was in my first year at university then, and, even though I'd known how frail he was, somehow I hadn't...I wasn't prepared. Losing him was such a shock. He was all I had, you see, and so when Victor proposed to me and told me that it was what Gramps would have wanted, I...' She ducked her head and looked away from Marco and then said in a low voice, 'I should have refused, but somehow I just couldn't imagine how I would manage on my own. I was so afraid...such a coward.'

'So it was a marriage of necessity?' Marco shrugged dismissively. 'Was he good in bed?'

It continued to irk Marco to have to admit that his direct and unsubtle challenge to Emily had sprung from a sudden surge of physical jealousy that the thought of her with another man had aroused. But then sexual jealousy wasn't an emotion he'd ever previously had to deal with. Sex was sex, a physical appetite satisfied by a physical act. Emotions didn't come into it and he had never seen why they should. He still didn't. And he still had no idea what had made him confront her like that, or what had driven such an out-of-character fury at the thought of her with another man, even though she had had yet to become his. It had caught him totally off guard when he had seen the sudden shimmer of suppressed tears in her eyes. At first he'd wanted to believe they were caused by her grief at the breakdown of her marriage, but to his shock, she had told him quietly:

'Our marriage...our relationship, in fact, was never physically consummated.'

Marco remembered how he had struggled not to show his astonishment, perhaps for the first time in his life recognising that what he had needed to show wasn't the arrogant disbelief so often evinced by his grandfather, but instead restraint and patience, to give her time to explain. Which was exactly what she had done, once she had silently checked that he wasn't going to refuse to believe her.

'I was too naïve to realise at first that Victor making no attempt to approach me sexually might not be a... because of gentlemanly consideration for my inexperience,' she continued. 'And then even after we were married—I didn't want him, you see, so it was easy for me not to question why he didn't want to make love to me. If I hadn't lived such a sheltered life, and I'd spent more time with people my own age, things would probably have been different, and I'd certainly have been more aware that something wasn't right. But as it was, it wasn't until I...I found him in bed with someone else that I realised—'

'He had a mistress,' Marco interrupted her, his normal instinct to question and probe reasserting itself.

There was just the merest pause before she told him quietly, 'He had a lover, yes. A *male* lover,' she emphasised shakily.

'I should have guessed, of course, and I suspect poor Victor thought that I had. He treated me very much as a junior partner in our relationship, like a child whom he expected to revere him and accept his superiority. For me to find him in bed with one of his young students was a terrible blow to his pride. He couldn't forgive me for blundering in on them, and the only way I could forgive myself for being so foolish was to insist that we divorce. At first he was reluctant to agree. He belonged more to my grandfather's generation than to his own, I suspect. He couldn't come to terms with his sexuality, which was why he had tried to conceal it within a fake marriage. He refused to say why he couldn't be open about his sexual nature. He got very angry when I tried to talk to him about it and suggested that, for his own sake, he should accept himself. The truth was, as I quickly learned, that to others his sexuality was not the secret he liked to think. There was no valid reason why he should have hidden it, but he was just that kind of man.

'I'd been left a bit of money by my grandfather, so I came to London and got a job. I'd always been interested in interior design, so I went back to college to get my qualifications and then a couple of years ago, after working for someone else's studio, I set up in business on my own. I wanted a fresh start and to get away from people who had known...about Victor. They must have thought me such a fool for not realising. I felt almost as though I was some kind of freak... Married, but not married.'

'And a virgin?' Marco added.

'Yes,' Emily agreed, before continuing, 'I wanted to be somewhere where no one was going to make assumptions about me because of my marriage.'

Their food arrived before Marco had the chance ask her about the man whom he assumed must have eventually taken her virginity. But he wondered about him. And envied him?

Marco frowned now, not wanting to remember the fierce sense of urgency to make Emily totally his that had filled him then and that had continued to hold him in its grip even when he had ultimately possessed her.

He walked back to the bed whilst Emily watched him, her heart thumping unsteadily into her ribs. They had been lovers for almost three years, but Marco still had the same effect on her as he had done the first time she had seen him; the impact of his male sexuality was such that it both enthralled and overwhelmed her, even now when she could feel the pain of the emotional gulf between them almost as strongly as she felt her own desire. When they had first met, she had immediately craved him, though she hadn't known then that her desire for him would enslave her emotionally as well as physically. And if she had, would she have behaved differently? Would she still have turned on the heels of those expensive Gina shoes she'd been wearing and have tip-tapped away from him as fast as she could?

Emily was glad of the night's shadows to conceal the pain in her eyes—a pain that would betray her if Marco saw it. It had been just before Christmas when she had first noticed that he'd seemed irritated and preoccupied, retreating into himself and excluding her. She had thought at first he must have some big business deal going down, but now she was beginning to fear that the source of his discontent might be her and their relationship. If his withdrawal had begun in the months immediately after the accident in which Marco had lost both his parents, she might have been able to tell herself that it was his grief that was responsible. After all, even a man who prided himself on being as unemotional as Marco did was bound to suffer after such a traumatic event. However, the first thing he had done on his return was take her to bed, without saying a word about either the funeral or his family, making love to her fiercely and almost compulsively.

Marco had rarely talked to her about his childhood, and never about his family. That had suited her perfectly at first. She had looked on her relationship with him initially as a necessary transition for her from *naïveté* to experience, a much-needed bridge across the chasm dividing her past from her future, her passport to a new life and womanhood. Because even then she had hoped that, one day, she would find a true partner: a man with whom she could share her life; a man to whom she could give her love as freely as he would give his to her; a man with whom she could have children.

But how foolish she had been, how recklessly unaware of the danger she had been placing herself in. It had simply never occurred to her then that she might fall in love with Marco! He had been totally open with her about the way he lived his life and what he looked for in his relationships: whilst they were together she could rely on his total fidelity, but once their relationship was over, it would be over, *full stop*. He wanted no emotional commitment from her nor should she expect one from him. And most important of all, she must not get pregnant.

'But what if there's an accident and...?' she asked him uncertainly.

He stopped her immediately

'There will not be any accidents,' he told her bluntly. 'With modern methods of contraception, there is no reason why there should be an accident—if you have any reason to suspect there may have been, then you must ensure that the situation is rectified without any delay.'

She wanted him too much to allow herself to admit how shocked she was by his cold-hearted attitude. Instead, she told herself that it didn't really matter, since she wanted to wait to have her children until she had found the right father for them and the right man for her.

Marco had pursued her so relentlessly and determinedly and she had wanted him so badly that the truth was whatever doubts she might have had had been totally overwhelmed by the sexual excitement they generated between them. For the first time in her life she knew the true meaning of the word 'lust'. Her every waking thought—and most of her dreams too—were of him and what it was going to be like when he took her to bed.

Thanks to the kindness of her first employer, who had passed on to her some of his clients when she had started up on her own, she had established a good and profitable business, which earned her enough to enable her to visit one of London's more exclusive lingerie shops in search of the kind of discreetly provocative underwear her fevered imagination hoped would delight and excite Marco. Within a week of meeting him, she had taken to wearing the seductively skimpy bits of silk and lace to work, just in case Marco appeared and insisted on taking her to his apartment to consummate their relationship. It made her smile now to remember how sensually brave she had felt. And the things she had imagined might happen…

Her fevered imaginings had come nowhere near to matching the reality of her reaction to Marco's skilled lovemaking. He had undressed her slowly and expertly, in her pretty bedroom in her small Chelsea house, almost teasing her by making her quivering body wait for his touch. And then, even when he had finally touched her, his caresses had been tantalisingly—tormentingly—light, the merest brush of fingertips and lips, which had fed her longing for something darker and far more intimate. Just thinking about it now was enough to make her heart turn over inside her chest and make her go weak with longing for him. She remembered how she had tried to show him her impatience, but Marco had refused to be hurried. His lips had teased the tight flesh of her nipples, and his fingers had brushed her belly and then stroked lightly against her thighs whilst she had sighed with arousal. His hand had parted her thighs, his fingers stroking over her sex, his touch making her want to moan out aloud with hunger.

He had just begun to kiss her more passionately when the telephone beside her bed had begun to ring. Idiotically she had answered it, only to discover that the caller was one of her more difficult clients who wanted to discuss her idea for a new makeover. By the time she had got rid of the client, Marco had got dressed, smiling urbanely at her, but making it clear that he was *not* going to take second place to her business.

The incident had shown her that he would always have it his way and she had not made the same mistake again. Or had her mistake been in tailoring her working life around him? That hadn't been just for his benefit though; she had wanted to make room in her life for him. Something deep inside her, which she had only recently begun to recognise, was showing her that she was the kind of woman who secretly longed to be the hub of her family, both as a wife and a mother. She didn't want to be on the other side of the world helping a client to choose the right paint shade for her new décor, leaving her partner to come home from work to an empty house and an empty bed. When she did marry and have children, she wanted to be the one those children ran to with their small everyday triumphs and hurts. She enjoyed her work, and she was proud of the ways in which she had built up her business, but she knew that it was the pleasure of creating a happy environment for those she loved that truly motivated her, rather than the excitement of a large bank balance.

Nonetheless, Marco was the kind of man who enjoyed a challenge, and it had made her feel a bit better when, later, he'd admitted how much he had ached for her that night. It could not have been any more than she had ached for him, she knew. Less than three months after they had first met he had asked her to move in with him. And then they'd had their first quarrel, when she had discovered that he'd expected her to give up her business, saying imperiously that he would give her an allowance that would more than compensate her for any loss of income.

'I want to be with you,' she told him fiercely. 'But I will not give up my financial independence, Marco. I don't want your money.'

'So what do you want?' he demanded, almost suspiciously.

'You,' she told him simply, and their quarrel was forgotten, as he was appeased by her bold request—or so she had thought. It was only later she had learned that, far from respecting her for refusing his money and his expensive gifts, he was both suspicious of her and slightly contemptuous. Perhaps if she had heeded the warning that knowledge had given her, she would not be in the situation she was now.

CHAPTER THREE

THEY had shared such wonderful months. Marco worked hard, but he believed in enjoying the good things in life as well. He had the air of someone who was used to the best of everything. But whilst sometimes she had deplored his inbuilt arrogance, and had teased him gently about it, Emily admitted that she'd enjoyed the new experiences to which he'd introduced her. Marco had taken her out several times a week but, best of all, as a lover he hadn't just fulfilled her fantasies, he had exceeded them and then taken her with him to realms of sexual discovery and delight she had never imagined existed.

Within weeks of them becoming lovers she had been so exquisitely sensually aware of him that just the touch of his hand on her arm, or the look in his eyes when he'd needed her to know that he wanted her, had been enough to have her answering with a look of her own that said, 'Please take me to bed.' Not that they had always made it to a bed. Marco was a demanding and masterful lover who enjoyed leading the way and introducing her to new pleasures, sometimes taking her quickly and erotically in venues so nearly public that she blushed guiltily af-terwards when she remembered, sometimes ensuring their lovemaking lasted all night—or most of the day. And she had been an eager pupil, wanting him more as time went by, rather than less, as her own sexuality and confidence grew under his expert guidance.

The first Christmas they had shared together, Marco had given her a beautiful three-carat diamond, which he had told her she could have set in the ring design of her choice. Emily knew that it had surprised him when she'd asked him instead to make a donation to her favourite children's charity.

Marco hadn't said anything, but on her birthday he had taken her away to a romantic hideaway and made love to her until she had cried with joy. He had then presented her with a pair of two-carat diamond ear-studs, telling her, 'I have sent a cheque of equivalent value to your charity.'

It had been then that she had realised that she had done the unforgivable and fallen in love with him!

Yes, how very foolish she had been to do that. He was back in their bed now, but lying with his back to her. Outside, the gale that had begun to blow earlier last evening hurled itself against the windows as the storm increased in force.

Normally, the knowledge that she was safe and warm inside whilst outside ice-cold rain sleeted down would have given her a feeling of delicious security, especially if she was wrapped up tightly in Marco's arms. But of course she wasn't. *Was* he tiring of her?

Marco could hear Emily breathing softly behind him. His body craved the release physically possessing her would bring, and why shouldn't he have it? he asked himself. He had already decided on the financial amount he was prepared to give Emily in recognition of the time they had spent together—a very generous one. So generous that he felt justified now in thinking that he might as well continue to enjoy her. He couldn't entirely get his head around the fact that he wanted Emily still, when other women who had shared his bed before her—women who had been so much more experienced and sexually enterprising—had bored him so quickly. It surprised him even more that he had actually grown to want her company away from bed, to the extent of talking to her about his business, and allowing her to persuade him to make donations to her precious charity. He had scarcely even been able to believe it at first when he had found out how much of her modest income she gave to helping a foundation set up to help London's deprived children and teenagers. Emily would not approve of his grandfather's refusal to do anything to help the least wealthy of Niroli's people; King Giorgio did not see the sense of educating the poor to expect more out of life than he felt the island could give them.

No, Emily was definitely not suitable material as the King of Niroli's mistress. But, of course, he was not yet King. Purposefully Marco moved, swiftly reaching for her, briefly studying the outline of her figure, the curve of her breast making him remember how perfectly its softness fitted into his cupped hand. As always, the strongly sensual core of his nature reacted to Emily's nearness. He might have already made love with her a thousand times and more during their relationship, but that couldn't dim the fierce desire he felt now. Some-where deep down within himself he registered the potential danger of such a compulsion and then dismissed it. He intended to end his affair with her before he left for Niroli. He'd make sure that no vestige of longing for her would cling to his memory or his senses; he was determined she would be easily replaced in his bed. If his body recognised something in her that was particularly enjoyable, that did not mean that he was in danger of craving her for ever. He relaxed as he dismissed as ludicrous the notion that he was at any kind of risk from his desire for her.

The moment Marco touched her, Emily could feel her

body becoming softly compliant, outwardly and inwardly, where it tightened and ached, the desire for him that never left her ramping up with a swift familiarity. Marco pushed back the bedclothes; a thin beam of moonlight silvered her breast, plucking sensually at her nipple and tightening it for his visual appreciation and enjoyment. He traced its circle of light, making her shiver with pleasure whilst her back began to arch in an age-old symbolic female gesture of enticement in offering her flesh to her lover.

Marco's hands tightened on Emily's slender form. She looked up at him, her eyes wide with arousal and excitement as she reached up to him. All that mattered to him right now was his possession of her, his pleasure found in witnessing her ecstasy as he took her and filled her, losing himself in her and taking her with him. His need pounded through him, obliterating everything else. He pushed aside her hair and kissed the side of her neck where he knew his touch reduced her to quivering delight, his hands cupping her breasts, kneading them erotically, his erection already stiff against her thigh where he had locked her to him with one out-flung leg.

Emily smiled to herself. Sex to Marco meant physically claiming every bit of her. Even when he kissed her casually, he liked to have her body in full contact with his. Not that she minded. Not one little bit! She loved the possessive sensuality of his desire for her. It was only in his arms, here like this, that she was truly able to let her real feelings have their head, instead of fighting to preserve the protective air of calm control she normally used to conceal them. When he made love to her, Marco never held back from showing her his passion for her, which, in turn, allowed her to set free her equally passionate longing for him. There was sometimes something almost pagan in the way they made love that secretly sometimes half shocked her. Always attuned to Marco's moods, tonight she sensed an urgency about him that added an extra edge to her own growing sexual tension. She gave a soft whimper as his mouth took the silvered ache of her nipple and his hand accepted the invitation of her open legs.

Once in their early days as lovers, sensing her uncertainty and slight awkwardness with her own sexuality, he had relaxed her with an evening of champagne and slow lovemaking, before coaxing her to let him position both of them where she could see the reflection of their naked bodies in a mirror. Then carefully, and with breathtakingly deliberate sensuality, he had revealed to her the mysteries of her own sex, showing her its desire-swollen and flushed outer lips, caressing them so that she could see her body's reaction to his touch, sliding his fingertip the whole length of her wetness before focusing on the tight, excited and oh-so-sexually-sensitive flesh of her clitoris. He had brought her to orgasm there in full view of her own half-shocked, half-excited gaze.

But she'd had her own sweet revenge later, turning the tables on him by exploring him with shamelessly avid hands and lips, spreading apart his heavily muscled male thighs so that she could know the reality of his sex with every one of her senses.

Now, as his fingers probed her wetness, she rose up eager to accept their gift of pleasure. But, for once, he didn't seem inclined to draw out their love-play, instead suddenly groaning and reaching for her, covering her and thrusting powerfully and compulsively into her, as though he couldn't get enough of her, driving them both higher, deeper, closer to the sanctuary that waited for them.

Instinctively Emily clung to him, riding the storm with him, welcoming him and sharing its turbulence.

Marco could feel an unfamiliar urgency possessing him and compelling him, demanding that he thrust harder and deeper. Emily shuddered beneath the intensity of his passion, immediately responsive to it. Her nails raked his back where his flesh lay tightly against his muscles, inciting him to fill her and complete her. The sensation of the tight heat of her wetness as it gripped and caressed him flooded everything but his ability to respond to her sensual urging from his mind. A primitive need surged through him. It had been some time since he'd last used a condom when they had sex; their relationship was of a long enough duration for him to know that there were no health reasons for him to do so, and that Emily was on the pill. Also, he knew how much she herself loved the skin-on-skin contact of their meshing bodies.

Was Marco aware of how deeply he was penetrating her, Emily wondered dizzily, or how intense and primeval a pleasure it was for her, as surges of sensation built, promising her orgasm? Did he know that when he came he would spill so very close to her womb? Did he know how much she wanted him; how much she ached now, right now, for him? She gave a low soft, almost tormented cry as her orgasm began, clutching at Marco, her head thrown back in pagan ecstasy as her pleasure shuddered through her, only to intensify into a second spiral of even greater intensity that shook her in its grip and melted her bones as Marco came hotly inside her.

Emily blinked fiercely. What they had just shared had been incredibly close and physically satisfying. Emotional tears slid down her face. Surely it wasn't possible for Marco to make love to her like this and not be in love with her? Perhaps the change she had sensed in him was because he *was* falling in love with her and he was reluctant to admit it? Tenderness for him, and for the vulnerability she knew he would never admit to, stole through her. She snuggled closer to him, warmed by his body and the intimacy they had shared, and most of all by the glow of the hope growing inside her. She would teach him that their love would make him stronger, not weaker; she would show him, as she'd tried to do all along, that *he* was what mattered to her and not the things he could give her. Marco had never told her why he was so adamant that love wasn't something he believed in or wanted, and she assumed that it must be because as a very young man he had been badly hurt and had vowed never to fall in love again. In a man as proud as Marco, such a wound would go very deep. Although people had been quick to gossip to her about him when she'd first met him, and about the stream of glamorous women who'd graced his arm and his bed before her, no one seemed to know much about his life before he had come to London. Marco was fiercely protective of his past and his privacy, and Emily had learned very early on in their relationship how shuttered he could be when she tried to get him to open up to her. So, it had to mean something that they were still together, Emily told herself sleepily. Why shouldn't that something be that he had fallen in love with her without even realising it?

CHAPTER FOUR

'AND I want the whole place to—y'know—like be totally me. So there'll have to be plenty of pink and loads of open-plan storage for my shoes. All my fans know that I'm a total shoe-freak.'

Emily was finding it a struggle to focus on what her latest client was saying, and not just because the reality-TV star's views on how she wanted her apartment designed and decorated were depressingly banal, she admitted.

The truth was that her normal professionalism and love of her work had in recent weeks become shadowed by her almost constant tiredness and bouts of sickness that had to be the legacy of a virus that she didn't seem to have entirely thrown off.

The reality-TV star was pouting and looking impatiently at her watch.

'Do we have to do this?' she asked the PR executive who was 'minding' her. 'I thought you said that I'd be doing a TV documentary about me designing my new apartment, not doing boring stuff like listening to some decorator.'

Whilst the PR girl attempted to soothe her charge, Emily moved discreetly out of earshot. Marco had left early this morning for his office whilst she had still been asleep, leaving her a scrawled note on the kitchen counter to say that he had some work he needed to catch up on. There was nothing particularly unusual in his early start. As an entrepreneur he often needed to be at his desk while the Far-Eastern financial markets were dealing. But today, for some reason, Emily was conscious of a deep-rooted emotional need to see him, be with him. Why? Surely not just because he had left without waking her to give her a good-morning kiss? A little rueful, she shook her head over her own neediness, determined to dismiss it. But it refused to go away, if anything sharpening so that it became a fierce ache of anxious longing. She looked at her watch. It was almost lunchtime. In the early stages of their relationship before Marco had told her that he wanted her to move in with him, she had, with some trepidation, and with what she had considered to be great daring, taken him up on what she had believed to be a casual invitation to drop in on him if she was ever passing by his office. Emily's heart started to go faster in a sudden flurry of excited little beats, the grating sound of the TV star's voice fading, as she recalled how she had taken him up on his offer…

Marco's initial greeting of her had not been welcoming. 'You were beginning to annoy me with the way you've been deliberately keeping me waiting,' he told her flatly, after his secretary had shown her into his office and then discreetly left them alone together. 'In fact you were beginning to annoy me so much that if you left it another day to visit, you wouldn't have got past my receptionist,' he added arrogantly.

His verbal attack stunned her into a bewildered silence, which had her shaking her head in mute protest.

'If you think that by holding me off, and making me wait, you'll—'

'Why on earth should I do that?' Emily interrupted him, too shocked by his accusations to recognise what she was giving away until she saw the satisfaction gleaming in his eyes and he came towards her saying softly,

'Well, in that case, we've got some catching up to do, haven't we?' When he took hold of her hands and drew her towards him, she was trembling so much with arousal and excitement that he smiled again. Not that he wasn't equally turned on; he told her with sexy intent in between his kisses how much he wanted her and what that wanting was doing to him.

If his telephone hadn't rung, Emily suspected that she would have let him make love to her there and then in his office. She certainly hadn't tried to stop him when he had unfastened her blouse and peeled back the lace of her bra, exposing her breast to his glitteringly erotic gaze and the skilled touch of his hand. His lips had been on its creamy slope when his phone had rung. She had tried to straighten her clothes as he'd answered the call, but he had stopped her, very deliberately tracing the tight excitement of her nipple with one lazy fingertip whilst he'd spoken to his caller. Emily could feel her body tightening now as she remembered the effect the highly charged atmosphere between them had had on her, and the contrast between the calm, businesslike tone of his voice and the deliberately sensual way in which he had been touching her. By the time he had finished his call she had been aching with longing for him to take their intimacy to its natural conclusion, but instead he had released her, fastening her top and then saying calmly,

'Come on, let's go out and have some lunch.'

She hadn't known him well enough then, of course, to realise that his deliberate arousal of her had been his way of punishing her for what he believed had been her attempt to control their relationship, and him.

Those had been such achingly sweet times, when they had first met. Suddenly she yearned to recapture them. Impulsively, she went over to the PR girl and told her firmly, 'I'm afraid I have to go. You've got my e-mail address if you need to contact me.' Emily suspected from the look the TV star was giving her that she wasn't going to get any commission for this project. But then, she told herself, right now being with Marco was more important to her than anything.

Marco stood beside his desk in the sleek modern office suite where he conducted his global financial affairs. When he had left Niroli vowing to make his own mark in the world without his royal status, his grandfather had laughed at him and warned him that he would be back within six months with his tail between his legs. He could have been, Marco admitted: at twenty-two, his belief in his own abilities had been far greater than his financial astuteness; initially he had lost money as he'd played the international stock markets. But, just when he had begun to fear the worst, his mother's great aunt had died in Italy, leaving him a substantial amount of money. A second stroke of luck had led him to come to the attention of one of the City's richest entrepreneurs, who had taken Marco under his wing, teaching him to use his skills and hone his killer financial instincts. Within a year, Marco had doubled his inheritance, and within five years he had become a billionaire in his own right.

Emily had designed Marco's office for him. On the traditional partners' desk she had given him as a birthday gift, there was a silver-framed photograph of the two of them, taken on the anniversary of their first year together, before the death of his parents. Marco now studied it: he saw Emily looking up at him, her expression filled with laughter and desire, whilst his own was shadowed and half hidden. But then, Marco knew, his eyes reflected the physical hunger he had seen in hers, just as the positioning of their bodies mirrored one another. Emily was gazing at him with open happiness in her eyes, because she knew he was a wealthy man and a skilled lover.

'Niroli's kings receive love, Marco,' his grandfather had told him when he was a young adolescent, 'they do not give it. They are above other, weaker men, and they do not try to turn physical desire into mawkish sentiment like other, lesser men. They do not need to. You are maturing fast and you will discover very soon that your royal status will draw to you your pick of the world's most beautiful and predatory women. They will give you their bodies but, in return, they will try to demand that you give them money and status. They will try to scheme, lie and cheat their way into your bed, and if you are foolish enough to let them they will present you with bastard sons who will become permanent remind-ers of your own folly and permanent dangers to Niroli's throne. It is not so many centuries ago that a newly crowned sultan would order the death or the castration of all his many male half-siblings in order to prevent them from trying to take his place. You're welcome to taste the pleasure of the women who offer themselves to you as much as you wish, but remember what I have told you. Ultimately you will make a necessary dynastic marriage with a young woman of royal and unimpeachable moral virtue, and she will give you your legitimate heirs. Your only heirs, if you are wise, Marco.'

Well, he had been wise, hadn't he? Marco told himself grimly. And he intended to continue to be so. He looked down at the letter on the desk in front of him. It had arrived the previous day, its royal crest and the Nirolean stamp immediately marking it out as the reason why he was in the office so early this morning. It was from his grandfather, setting out the final details of his abdication plans. The people of Niroli, King Giorgio had written, were already being encouraged to expect Marco's return and to welcome him as their new ruler. He needed to speak with his grandfather. But protocol meant that, yesterday, Marco had patiently followed an archaic, convoluted procedure, which had ensured that none of the ancient statesmen who surrounded his grandfather would have their pride dented, before finally arranging to speak directly to the king. Marco intended to make a clean sweep of these elderly statesmen once he was on the throne. His plan was to bring a forward-thinking modern mindset to the way Niroli was ruled, via courtiers of his own generation who shared his way of thinking. In fact, this new regime was something he already had in hand after a few discreet one-to-one telephone calls.

He looked at his watch: in another twenty minutes exactly, the telephone on his desk would ring and the Groom of the Chamber would announce in his quavering voice that he was going to connect him to his grandfather. Marco sighed. The elderly courtier was hard of hearing, as indeed was his grandfather, although King Giorgio denied it! Marco had a rueful fondness for his older relative, and he knew that Giorgio had a grudging respect for him, but he also knew that both of them were far too similar to ever be willing to be open about those feelings. Instead they tended to conform to the roles they had adopted in Marco's teenage years, when his grandfather had been the disapproving disciplinarian and he had been the rebellious black sheep. He checked the time again. All this simply so that he could assure his grandfather that he would be returning to Niroli just as soon as he had dealt with his outstanding business in London, something that should have been a simple matter of a quick phone call rather than this long-drawn-out ceremonial.

The part of Marco's outstanding business that concerned Emily was of course something he did not intend to discuss with the old king. He estimated that it would be a few weeks yet before he would be ready to leave, and he had already decided that there would be no sense in telling Emily their relationship had to end until then. One single clean cut, with no possibility of any come-backs, was the best way to deal with the situation. He would tell her they were finished and that he was leaving the country—and that was all. He had taken her to his bed as plain Marco Fierezza and he saw no point in revealing his royal status to her now. She had known him as her lover and a wealthy entrepreneur, not as the future King of Niroli. It was true that she might at some future point come to discover who he was—the paparazzi took a keen interest in the Royal House of Niroli—but by then their lives would be entirely separate. Their relationship had never been intended to end in commitment. He had told her that right from the start. But they had been together for almost three years, when previously he had become bored with his girlfriends within three months. Marco shrugged away the dry inner voice pointing out things to him he didn't want to acknowledge. So, sexually they might have been well suited, or maybe at thirty-six the raw heat of his sex drive was cooling and he demanded less stimulation and variety, which made him content to accept a familiar physical diet? It would do him good to get out of that kind of sexual rut, he told himself coolly.

It would do them both good. Marco started as, out of nowhere, a sharply savage spear of sexual jealousy stabbed through him. What was this? Why on earth should he feel such a gut-wrenching surge of fury at the thought of Emily moving on to another man? His mouth compressed. His concern was for Emily, and not for himself. She was after all the vulnerable one, not him. Emily's sexual past was very different from his own, and because of that—and only that, he assured himself—he was now experiencing a completely natural concern that she was not equipped to deal with a lover who might not treat her as well as he had done.

Marco looked at her picture, reluctantly remembering the first time he had possessed her. He'd planned to surprise her, but in the end she had been the one who had surprised him...

He had seen how excited she'd been when he'd walked into her shop and told her that he was taking her away for a few days, and that she would need her passport. When he'd picked her up later that day, he had seen quite plainly in her expression how much she'd wanted him. As he had wanted her.

He had been totally—almost brutally, some might have said—honest with her about the fact that he had no time for the emotional foolishness of falling in love. He had informed her calmly that he had ended previous relationships for no other reason than that his girlfriends had told him that they were falling in love with him. Emily had greeted his announcement with equal calm. Falling in love with him wasn't something she planned to do, she had assured him firmly. She was as committed to their relationship being based on their sexual need for one another as he was himself, she had smiled, adding that this suited her perfectly, and Marco had felt she was speaking the truth.

He had booked the two of them into a complex on a small private island that catered exclusively for the rich and the childfree. Everything about the location was designed to appeal to lovers and to cocoon them in privacy, whilst providing a discreet service.

The individual villas that housed the guests were set apart from the main hotel block, each with its own private pool. Meals could be taken in the villas or in the Michelin-starred restaurant of the hotel, where there was also an elegant bar and nightclub.

Amongst the facilities included for the guests' entertainment were diving and sailing, and visits to the larger, more built-up neighbouring islands could be arranged by helicopter if guests wished.

They had arrived late in the afternoon, and had walked through the stunningly beautiful gardens. Marco recalled now how Emily had reached out to hold his hand, her eyes shining with awed wonder as they had paused to watch the breathtaking swiftness of the sunset. He remembered, too, how he had been unable to resist taking her in his arms and kissing her, and how that kiss had become so intimate it had left Emily trembling.

They had returned to their villa, undressing one another eagerly and speedily, sharing the shower in the luxuriously equipped bathroom. Emily's physical response to him had been everything Marco had hoped it would be and more. She had held nothing back, matching him touch for touch and in intimacy until he had started to penetrate her. It had caught him off guard to have her tensing as he thrust fully into her, believing she was as eager to feel the driving surge of his body within hers as he was to feel her hot, wet flesh tightening around him.

At first he had assumed she was playing some kind of coy game with him, mistakenly thinking that it would excite him if she assumed a mock-innocent hesitancy. His frustration had made him less perceptive than he might otherwise have been, and more impatient, so he had ignored the warning her body had been giving him and had thrust strongly again. This time it had taken the small muffled sound that had escaped past her rigid throat muscles to make him realise the truth: she was still a virgin.

His first reaction had been one of savage anger, fuelled by the toxic mingling of male frustration and the blow to his own pride that was caused by the fact that he hadn't guessed the truth. Sex with an inexperienced virgin—and the potential burden of responsibility that carried, both physical and emotional—was something he just had not wanted.

'What the hell is this?' he swore. 'Okay, I know about your marriage, but I would have thought that…if only because of that…'

'That *what?* That I'd jump on the first man I could find?' Emily retaliated sharply. But beneath that sharpness he caught the quiver of uncertainty in her voice, and his anger softened into something that caught at his throat, startling him with its intensity.

'Well, it did cross my mind,' she told him. 'But in the end I was too much of a moral coward to go through with it. Blame my grandfather, if you wish, but the thought of having sex with a man I didn't truly want, just to get rid of my virginity, has made it harder rather than easier for me to find a man I did want enough.'

Marco shrugged dismissively, not wanting to have to deal with his own unfamiliar feelings, never mind hers!

'If you're expecting me to be pleased about this, then let me tell you—'

'You don't need to tell me anything, Marco,' she had stopped him determinedly. 'It's rather obvious what you feel.'

'I don't know what you're thinking, or hoping for,' he told her, ignoring her comment, 'but, despite what you may want to believe, the majority of sexually mature men do not fantasise about initiating a virgin! I certainly don't. The reason I brought you here was so that we could indulge our need for one another as two people starting from the same baseline. For me, that means we share matching physical desires for one another and awareness of our own sexual wants and expectations.'

'I'm sorry if you feel that I've let you bring me here under false pretences,' Emily told him, admitting, 'Maybe I should have said something to warn you?'

'Maybe?'

The scorn in his voice made her flinch visibly. 'I didn't want to play the I'm-still-a-virgin card for the reasons you've just mentioned yourself,' she defended. 'I didn't want it to be an issue and, besides, I wasn't even sure that you'd notice.'

Marco remembered how she had coloured up hotly when he had looked at her in disbelief.

'I really am sorry,' she told him apologetically.

'*You're* sorry? I'm so damn frustrated…' he began.

'Me, too,' Emily interrupted him with such candour that he felt his earlier irritation evaporating.

'Frustrated, but virginal and apprehensive?' he felt bound to point out.

'Yes, but not one of those has to remain a permanent state, does it?' she responded.

'You trust me to deal effectively with all three?'

'I trust you to make it possible for *us* to deal with all three,' she corrected him softly. 'I'm a woman who believes that participation in a shared event makes for mutual enjoyment, even if right now in this particular venture I am the junior partner.'

He wasn't used to being teased, or to sharing laughter in an intimate relationship and, as he quickly discovered, shared laughter had its own aphrodisiacal qualities.

He made love to her with a slow intimacy which, he was the first to admit, had its own reward when in the end she showed him such a passionate response. It was she who urged him to move faster and deeper, until he was as lost in the pleasure they were sharing as she was. But not so lost that he couldn't witness the shocked look of delight widening her eyes as her orgasm gripped her…

What the hell was he doing, thinking about that now? It was over; they were over; or rather they soon would be.

Someone was knocking gently on his office door. Marco

frowned. He wasn't expecting anyone and he had expressly told his PA not to disturb him. He was still frowning when the door opened and Emily stepped through, smiling at him. It wasn't often that Marco was caught off guard by anything or anyone, but on this occasion...

'My meeting finished early,' he could hear Emily saying breezily, 'So I thought I'd come over and see if you were free for lunch?'

When he didn't answer her she closed the office door and came towards him, dropping her voice to a playfully soft tone as she told him, 'Or maybe we could forget the going-out and the lunch. Remember, Marco, how we used to...What's wrong?' she asked him uncertainly.

Her smile disappeared and Marco recognised that he had left it several seconds too late to respond appropriately to her arrival.

Normally, the fact that his timing was at fault would have been his main concern. But, for some reason, he found that, not only was he acutely aware that he had hurt and upset Emily, he was also suppressing an immediate desire to go to her and apologise. Apologise? Him? Marco was astounded by his own uncharacteristic impulse. He never apologised to anyone, for anything.

'Nothing's wrong,' he told her flatly, knowing that something was very wrong indeed for him to have felt like that. It couldn't be that he was feeling guilty, could it? a traitorous, critical inner voice suddenly challenged, pointing out: *After all, you've lied to her and you're about to leave her...*

She knew the ground rules, Marco answered it inwardly. That his own conscience should turn on him like this increased his irritation and, man-like, he focused that irritation on Emily, rather than deal with its real cause.

'Yes, there is,' Emily persisted. 'You were looking at me as though I'm the last person you want to see.'

'Don't be ridiculous. I just wasn't expecting to see you.' He flicked back the sleeve of his suit—handmade, it fitted him in such a way that its subtle outlining of his superb physique was a whispered suggestion caught only by those who understood. 'Look, I can't do lunch, I've got an important call coming through any time now, and after than I've got an appointment.' That wasn't entirely true, but there was no way he wanted Emily to suggest she wait around for him whilst he spoke with his grandfather. For one thing, he had no idea just how long the call would last and, for another… For another, he wasn't ready yet to tell Emily what she had to be told.

Because he wasn't ready yet to deny himself the pleasure of making love to her, his inner tormentor piped up, adding mockingly, *Are you sure that you will ever be ready?* He dismissed that unwanted thought immediately but its existence increased his ire. 'Mrs Lawson should have told you that I'd said I didn't want to be disturbed,' he informed Emily curtly.

She heard the impatience in his voice and wished she hadn't bothered coming. Marco's arrogance made him forget sometimes how easily he could hurt her, and she certainly had too much pride to stay here and let him see that pain.

'Mrs Lawson wasn't there when I came in.'

'Not there? She's my PA, for heaven's sake. Where the hell is she?'

'She'd probably just slipped off to the cloakroom, Marco. It isn't her fault,' Emily pointed out quietly. 'Look, I'm sorry if this isn't a good time.' She gave a small resigned sigh. 'I suppose I should have checked with you first before coming over.'

'Yes, you should have,' Marco agreed grimly. Any minute now the phone was going to ring and if he picked it up she was going to hear his grandfather's most senior aide's voice booming out as he tried to compensate for his own deafness, 'Is that you, Your Highness?' The Comte had never really accustomed himself to the effectiveness of modern communication systems and still thought his voice could only travel down the telephone line if he spoke as loudly as he possibly could.

Emily's eyes widened as she registered Marco's rejection and then she stood still staring blankly at him, the colour leaving her face. He was treating her as though she were some casual and not very welcome acquaintance.

'Don't worry about it. I'm sorry I disturbed you,' she managed to say, but she could hear the brittle hurt in her own voice. Right now, she wanted to be as far away from Marco and his damn office as she could get! She was perilously close to tears and the last thing she wanted was the humiliation of Marco seeing how much he'd wounded her. To her relief, she could hear sounds from the outer office suggesting that his PA had returned, enabling her to use the face-saving fib that she didn't want to have Mrs Lawson coming in to shoo her out. Emily opened the door and left, barely pausing to acknowledge the PA's surprise at seeing her, Emily hurried out of the office, her head down and her throat thick with unshed tears.

What was it with her? she asked herself wretchedly, five minutes later as she hailed a taxi. She wasn't a young girl with emotions so new and raw that she overreacted to every sucked-in breath! She was in her twenties and divorced, and she and Marco had been together for nearly three years, the intimacy of their sex life having given her an outward patina of radiant sensuality. It had been so palpable in the first year they'd been together, one of her clients had told her semi-jokingly, 'Now that you're with Marco you're going to start losing clients if you aren't careful.'

'Why?' Emily had asked.

'Jealousy,' had been the client's succinct answer.

Emily remembered how she had smiled with rueful acknowledgement. 'You mean, because I'm with Marco and they'd like to change places with me?' she had guessed.

'They may very well want to do that, but I was thinking more of their concerns that their husbands might be tempted by the creamy glow of sexual completion you're carrying around with you right now, Emily.'

Emily remembered she had blushed and made some confused denial, but the client had shaken her head and told her wisely, 'You can't deny or ignore it. That glow shimmers round you like a force-field and men are going to be drawn to you because of it. There is nothing more likely to make a man want a woman than her confident wearing of another man's sexual interest in her.'

She doubted that she still wore that magnetic sexual aura now, Emily admitted sadly. That was the trouble: when you broke the rules, it didn't only make you ache for what you didn't have, it also damaged what you did.

The taxi driver was waiting for her to tell him where she wanted to go. She leaned forward and gave him the address of Marco's apartment. *Marco's apartment*, she noted—for that was how she thought of it. Not as *their* apartment, even though he had invited her to make it over to suit her own tastes and had given her a lavish budget for its renovation. Material possessions, even for one's home that evoked deep-rooted attachments, were nothing without the right kind of emotions to surround them. Why had it had to happen? Why had she fallen in love with Marco? Why couldn't she have stayed as she was, thrillingly aware of him on the most intimate kind of sexual level, buoyed up by the intensity of their desire for one another, overwhelmed by relief and joy because he had brought her from the dark, wretched nowhere she'd inhabited after her divorce to the brilliant glittering landscape of unimaginable beauty that was the intimacy they shared together?

Why, why, why couldn't that have been enough? Why had she had to go and fall for him?

Emily shivered, sinking deeper into the seat of the taxi. And why, having fallen for him, did she have to torment herself by hoping that one day things would change, that one day he would look at her and in his eyes she would see his love for her? The hope that, one day, it would happen sometimes felt so fragile and so unrealistic that she was afraid for herself, afraid of her vulnerability as a woman who needed one particular man so badly she was prepared to cling to such a fine thread. But what else could she do? She could tell him, honestly, how she felt. Emily bit her lip, guiltily aware that she wasn't being open with him. Because she was afraid in case she lost him…Why was she letting herself be dragged down by these uncomfortable, painful thoughts and questions? Why did they keep on escaping from the place where she tried to incarcerate and conceal them? What kind of woman was she to live a lie with the man she loved? What kind of relationship was it when that man stated openly that there was no place for love in the life he wanted to live?

The taxi stopped abruptly, catching her off guard. She didn't really want to go up to the apartment, not feeling the way she was right now, but another person was already hurrying purposefully towards the taxi, wanting to lay claim to it.

Emily got out and paid her fare to the driver, shivering as she waited for her change. Her stomach had already begun its familiar nauseous churning—this time, it had to be a result of Marco's rejection of her appeal to him, though she had to admit she had also felt too nauseous to want any breakfast this morning. She was definitely beginning to feel slightly dizzy and faint as well as unwell now.

Psychosomatic, she told herself unsympathetically as she headed up to the apartment.

It had started to rain while Emily was getting out of the taxi. Yes, the miserable weather was adding to her feelings of lowness. Why couldn't she talk to Marco? They were lovers, after all, sharing the closest of physical intimacy. Physical intimacy—but they did not share any emotional intimacy. Emily's experiences as a child had made her wary of appearing needy. It was now second nature to her to hide the most vulnerable part of her true self. Only in Marco's arms, at the height of their shared passion, did she feel safe enough to allow her body to show him what was in her heart, knowing that he wasn't likely to be able to recognise it.

She let herself into the apartment, mutely aware of how empty and impersonal it felt, for all her attempts to turn it into a shared home.

'Yes, Grandfather, I do understand, but I cannot work miracles. It is impossible for me to return to Niroli before the end of the month as we had already tentatively agreed.' Marco managed to hold onto his temper as his grandfather's complaints grew louder, before finally interrupting to say dryly, 'Very well, then, I accept that whilst I had talked about the end of the month, you had not agreed to it. But that doesn't alter the fact that I cannot return sooner.'

The sound of his grandfather slamming down the receiver reverberated in Marco's eardrum. Replacing his own handset, he stood up and turned to look out of the window of his office. It was raining. In Niroli, the sun would be shining. Marco's grandfather was obviously furious that he had refused to give in and alter the timing of his return and bring his arrival on Niroli forward. But his grandfather's rage did not worry Marco. He was used to it and unaffected by it, apart from the fact that he too didn't like having his plans challenged. He looked irritably at his watch. He was hungry and very much

in need of the gentle calm of Emily's company. That, plus the
natural reserve that made her the kind of woman who was
never going to court the attention of the paparazzi, or expose
their relationship to the avid curiosity of others, were two
other major plus-points about her. But not quite as major as
the sensuality that spilled from her like sweetness from a
honeycomb, even if she didn't realise it.

The direction his thoughts were taking surprised him. It
was nonsense for him to be thinking about Emily like this
when he was about to end their relationship! Far better that
he focused on the things he didn't like about her, such as...
Such as the way she insisted on keeping professional com-
mitments even when he had made other plans. *Is that the only
criticism you can make of her?* an increasingly voluble and
irritating inner voice demanded sardonically. Marco sighed,
mentally acknowledging the irony of his own thoughts. Yes,
it was true that, in many ways, Emily was the perfect mistress
for the man he had been whilst he'd lived in London. But he
wasn't going to be that man for much longer.

When the time came for him to take a royal mistress, she
would have to have qualities that Emily did not possess. Chief
amongst those would be an accepting, possibly older husband.
This was an example of the kind of protocol at the royal court
of Niroli which, in Marco's opinion, kept it in the Edwardian
era. He certainly planned to bring about changes that would
benefit the people of Niroli rather than its king. But perhaps
there were certain traditions that were better retained. No,
Emily could not continue to be his lover, but even so he could
have responded better to her arrival in his office earlier, Marco
admitted. He could, for instance, have suggested that she go
ahead to one of their favourite restaurants and wait there for
him. It had, after all, been predictable that his grandfather
would lose his temper and end their conversation so abruptly,

once he realised that he wasn't going to get everything that he wanted.

Marco toyed with the idea of calling Emily now and suggesting that she meet him for a late lunch, but then decided against it. She wasn't the kind of woman who sulked or played silly games. But honesty compelled him to accept that some measure of compensatory behaviour on his part would be a good invest- ment. Ridiculously in many ways, given the length of time they had been together, just thinking about her triggered that familiar sharp ache of his desire for her. He picked up the phone and rang the number of her shop.

Her assistant answered his call, telling him, 'She isn't here, Marco. She rang a couple of minutes ago to say that she's going to spend the rest of the day working at the apartment. Poor Emily, she still isn't properly over that wretched virus, is she?'

Marco made a noncommittal reply. He himself was never in anything other than the very best of health, but right now his mood was very much in need of the soothing touch that only Emily could give. She had an unexpectedly dry sense of humour, which, allied to her intelligence and acute perception, gave her the ability to make him laugh, sometimes when he least felt like doing so. Not that her sense of humour or his laughter had been very much in evidence these last few weeks, he recognised, frowning a little over this recognition. It surprised him how sharp the need he suddenly felt to be with her was. It was amazing what a bit of guilt could do, he decided as he told his PA that he, too, would be spending the afternoon working at home.

The best way to smooth over any upsets, so far as Marco was concerned, was in bed, where he knew he could quickly make Emily forget about everything other than his desire for her and hers for him…

* * *

Emily scowled as she worried over the message she had just picked up from one of her clients. The lady in question was a good customer, but Emily had still felt slightly wary when she'd been asked a while ago to take on the complete renovation of a property in Chelsea.

'Darling, darling, Emily,' Carla Mainwearing had trilled, 'I am so in love with your perfect sense of style that I want you to choose everything and I am going to put the house totally in your hands.'

Knowing Carla as she did, Emily had taken this with a pinch of salt and had therefore insisted on having her work approved at every single stage. Now Carla had left her a message saying that she hated the colour Emily had chosen for the walls of the property's pretty drawing room, and that she wanted it completely redone—at Emily's expense. Emily recalled that Carla had previously sanctioned the colour of the paint. But discretion was called for in telling her this, so rather than phone Carla back she decided to e-mail instead. Her laptop was in the study she shared with Marco, as were her files, so she made her way there, firmly ignoring the leaden weight of her earlier disappointment at Marco's refusal to join her for lunch.

Five minutes later, she was standing immobile in front of the study's window, her laptop and original purpose of coming to the study forgotten, as she stared in shocked horror at the vellum envelope she was holding. Her hand, actually not just her hand but her whole body, was trembling violently, as she felt unable to move. Waves of heat followed by icy chill surged through her body and somewhere some part of her mind managed to register the fact that what she was suffering was a classic reaction to extreme shock. She could hardly see the address on the envelope now through her blurred vision, but the crest on its left-hand front corner stood out, its *royal* crest, followed by the address: *HRH Prince Marco of Niroli*…

She didn't hear Marco's key in the apartment door, she didn't even hear him calling out her name. Her shock was so great that nothing could penetrate it. It encased her in a kind of bubble, which only concentrated the torment of what she was suffering and branded it on her brain so that it could never be forgotten. It was only finally pierced by the sudden opening of the study door as Marco walked in, but of course there was no way his arrival could ease her pain. Instead she gripped the envelope even tighter, her voice high and tight as she said thinly, 'Welcome home, *Your Highness*. I suppose I ought to curtsey to you.'

She waited, praying that he would laugh and tell her that she had got it all wrong, that the envelope she was holding, addressing him as Prince Marco of Niroli, was some silly mistake.

CHAPTER FIVE

LIKE a tiny candle flame shivering vulnerably in the dark, her hope trembled fearfully. And then the look in Marco's eyes extinguished it as cruelly as a hand placed callously over the face of a dying person to stem their last breath. It was over. Now, in this minute, this breath of time, they were finished. Emily knew that without the need for any words, the pain of that knowledge slamming a crippling body-blow into her. Her stomach felt as though she had plunged down a hundred floors in a high-speed lift.

'Give that to me,' Marco demanded, taking the envelope from her.

'It's too late to destroy the evidence, Marco.' Emily told him brokenly. 'I know the truth now. And I know how you've lied to me all this time, pretending to be something you aren't, letting me think…' She dug her teeth in her lower lip to try to force back her own pain. 'Do you think I haven't read the newspapers? Do you think the people of Niroli know that their prince is a liar? Or doesn't lying matter when you're a member of the Royal House?' she challenged him wildly.

'You had no right to go through my desk,' Marco shot back at her furiously, his male loathing at being caught off guard and forced into a position in which he was in the wrong making him determined to find something he could accuse Emily of. 'I thought we had an understanding that our private papers were our personal property and out of bounds,' he told her savagely. 'I trusted you...'

Emily could hardly believe what she was hearing.

'Did you? Is that why you hid this envelope under everything else?' she challenged him, shaking her head in answer to her own question. 'No, you didn't trust me, Marco, and you didn't trust me because you knew that I couldn't trust you. And you knew that because you are a liar, and liars don't trust people because they know that they themselves cannot be trusted.' She not only felt sick, she also felt as though she could hardly breathe. 'Everything I thought I knew about you is based on lies, everything. You aren't just Marco Fierezza, you are Prince Marco of Niroli. You yourself are a lie, Marco...'

'You are taking this far too personally. The reason I concealed my royal status had nothing whatsoever to do with you. It was a decision I made before I met you. My identity as plain Marco Fierezza is as real to me as though I were not a prince. It has nothing to do with you,' he repeated.

'How can you say that? It has everything to do with me, and if you had any shred of decency or morals you would know that. How could you lie about who you are and still live with me as intimately as we have lived together?' she demanded brokenly. 'How could you live with yourself, knowing that others, not just me, believed you, accepted and gave you their trust, when all the time—'

'Stop being so ridiculously dramatic,' Marco demanded fiercely. 'You are making too much of the situation.'

'Too much?' Emily almost screamed the words at him. 'Too much, when I have discovered that you have deceived me for the whole time we've been together? When did you plan to tell me, Marco? Perhaps you just planned to walk away without telling me anything? After all, what do my feelings matter to you?'

'Of course they matter,' Marco stopped her sharply. 'And it was in part to protect them, and you, that I decided not to inform you of the change in my circumstances when my grandfather first announced that he intended to step down from the throne and hand it on to me.'

'To protect me?' Emily almost choked on her fury. 'Hand on the throne? Don't bother continuing, Marco. No wonder you told me when you first took me to bed that all you wanted was sex. You *knew* that was the only kind of relationship there could ever be between us! You *knew* that one day you would be Niroli's king. No doubt you are expected to marry a princess. Is she picked out for you already, your *royal* bride?'

'No.'

Emily shrugged disdainfully. 'There's no point in replying because, whatever you say, I can't believe you, not now.'

'Emily, listen to me. This has gone far enough. You are being ridiculous. I know you have had a bit of a shock, but...'

'A bit of a shock? *A bit of a shock?*'

When she whirled round and headed for the door, Marco demanded, 'Where are you going?'

'To pack my things,' Emily told him fiercely. 'I'm leaving, Marco, right now. I can't and won't stay here with you. I feel I don't know you any more, and right now I don't really want to.'

'Don't be stupid. Where will you go? This is your home.'

'No, this is *your* apartment, it has never been my home. As to where I will go, I have a home of my own—remember?' she challenged him.

Marco frowned. 'Your house in Chelsea? But your assistant is living there.'

'She was living there, but she moved in with her new partner at the weekend, not that it or anything else in my life is any business of yours, Your Highness. Or should it be Your Majesty?'

'Emily.' He reached for her but she started to pull away from him, a look of angry contempt in her eyes that infuriated him. She had accused him of deceit and duplicity, but what about her actions? What about the fact that she had gone through his private papers behind his back? Her accusations had stung his pride, and now suddenly recognising that control of the situation had been taken from him and that she was about to walk out on him awakened all his most deeply held, atavistic male feelings about her. She was his—his until he chose to end their relationship.

Emily's eyes widened in mute shock as his fingers closed round her wrist, imprisoning her, and she saw the familiar look of arousal darkening his eyes. 'Let go of me,' she snapped. 'You can't really expect...'

'I can't really expect what?'

He wasn't going to let her go, Emily realised. She felt a quiver of sensation run down her spine—and it wasn't fear.

'What is it that I can't expect, Emily?' he repeated silkily. 'Is it that I can't expect to take you to bed any more—is that what you were going to say? That I can't expect to touch you or hold you?'

She had edged towards the study door as he'd advanced, but before she could open it and escape Marco reached past her, kicking it shut. Then, he placed his hands on it either side of her so that she was caught between the door and him. A telltale spiral of excitement was sizzling through her, its presence within her reminding her of the early days of their affair, when just to know that Marco wanted her and intended to have her was enough to leave her quivering on the edges of erotic need and surrender. Just as she was doing now. She tried to vocalise her denial, not just of her own arousal but also of Marco's intentions, but the words were locked in her throat. Beneath the soft wool of her sweater she could feel the growing hardening of her nipples and the desire-heavy weight of her breasts. How long had it been since she had felt like this? How long had it been since Marco had shown her this side of himself? So long that she couldn't remember? So long that, because it was happening now, she couldn't resist his allure?

Her heart jerked around inside her chest as though it were suspended on a piece of elastic. The ache in her breasts curled down through her belly to taunt her sex and tease from it a throbbing pulse of excitement and longing. She realised that she should be horrified by the way she was reacting to him, in view of what she had now discovered, horrified and determined not to let him touch her, sickened by the thought of him touching her. But she also knew that she wasn't; instead she wanted him with a physical intensity that held her fast in an unfamiliar, almost violent grip.

'Is that what you wanted to say to me, Emily—that I can't make you want me any more, that I can't arouse you, that I can't do this…?' He lifted his hand and stroked a fingertip down the side of her neck and along her collar-bone, making her shudder in violent erotic delight. He had moved closer to her, so close that she could smell the familiar scent of his cologne and the aroused heat of his body. Was it *that,* with its powerful but subtle message of male sexuality, that was turning her boneless with aching longing for him, even while her mind was telling her that she should resist him, and that this was no way for her to behave if she truly wanted him to believe what she had said?

She should say something, tell him to stop; tell him that there was no point in this for either of them. But she knew that she wouldn't, just as she knew that some deep-rooted female part of her wanted this show of male dominance from him, wanted her own sense of fierce surging excitement, wanted and needed the pure, fierce searing heat of the mutual lust they had conjured up out of nowhere. She could quite easily have pushed past him, Emily knew, and she knew too that Marco would not try to stop her if she did. But the reality was that she didn't want to… The reality was that her body was possessed by an incendiary mix of anger and desire that took fire from Marco's determination to confront her with her own acceptance of his power to arouse her.

'But that would be a lie, wouldn't it?' Marco challenged her softly as he continued his relentless sensual assault, his lips brushing the bare flesh of her throat in between each word, imprisoning her in her own wild arousal.

'Wouldn't it?' he insisted as he slid his hand beneath her sweater and freed her breasts from the constriction of her bra. A low moan of unappeased longing bubbled in her throat as he fed her craving for his possession.

'You want more?' he demanded, his voice thickening and softening.

'No!' Emily lied. She could feel his hand cupping her breast and his fingertips stroking deliberately against her nipple again. She knew she couldn't hold out much longer against the dammed-up force of her own need. With a low sound of surrender, she reached blindly for him, drawing his head down towards her own, her lips parting for his kiss and the swift, exultant victory of his tongue.

She could feel the thick hardness of his manhood pressing against her body. In her mind's eye she visualised his naked body, familiar now after their years together, seeing behind her closed eyes the thick sheathing of smooth flesh over rigid muscle, where it rose from the dark silky thickness of hair. She could almost feel the smooth warmth of him, so enticingly supple to her touch, and so responsive to the caress of her fingers and her mouth. Fresh longing seized her. Impetuously she reached down between their bodies to touch him, spanning his length with the spread of her fingertips, and then stroking his thickness. A deep purr of satisfaction gathered in her throat as she felt him stiffen further and then pulse, becoming a moan of out-of-control urgency when she felt him tugging at the fastening of her skirt.

Not even in their early days together had she experienced this degree of intense need, she recognised. It was so much bolder than anything she remembered feeling before; bolder, and fiercer and hungrier—the sexual desire of a woman who must be satisfied.

The demoralising fear that had in recent weeks sucked from her any delight in their intimacy was as easily sloughed off by their shared passion as were their clothes, unwanted encumbrances that prevented her from taking all that she could. Marco was driving both of them to that place where they had no choice other than to plunge into the turbulent flood of the maelstrom together.

Emily's fingers trembled over and tugged at his shirt buttons and trouser fastenings, her endeavours deliberately interrupted by him when he raked his teeth against the sensitive thrust of her nipple, causing her to gasp and then moan, unable to do anything other than give in to the intensity of the sensation he was inflicting on her. When pleasure was this intense, she thought frantically, it bordered on the almost unendurable. And yet she wouldn't have wanted it any other way, wouldn't have wanted any other man, wouldn't have been able to reach this lack of inhibition with anyone else.

'You want me to stop?' Marco demanded. His breath cooled the aching flesh that had been tormented by his erotic caress, whilst the subtle touch of his fingertips continued to play on her nipple, increasing its dark, swollen call for the renewed heat of his mouth.

Emily couldn't speak, she could barely stand up any more. But she knew Marco knew she wanted no such thing. She ran her hands along his sweat-dampened naked torso, deliberately bending her head so that she could graze her tongue-tip along his skin and taste the tangy maleness of his flesh, whilst she breathed in his aphrodisiacal Marco-drenched scent. At times like this, just the smell of him was enough to make her go weak with lust.

The ache deep inside her tightened and burned with a heat that could only be slaked by the possession of Marco's hard flesh filling her and completing her. She could feel the small hungry ripples of sensation caused by her muscles as they tightened with the need to have him fill the empty, wanton place inside her.

'Now, Marco,' she urged him fiercely, 'now!'

When he still waited, she looked up at him. She could see the dangerous look in his eyes, the darkness that said he was on the verge of wanting to punish her and that he was challenging her, needing to force her to acknowledge his supremacy, his ability to control her desire, arouse it and then satisfy it. It was too late for her to try to play him at his own game and deny him his triumph by pretending that she didn't want him. Her own need was too great and too immediate. She would have to punish herself later for her weakness. Right now, no price was too high to pay for the satisfaction her body craved. She had tried to resist…

'Now!' she repeated.

For a second, she thought he was going to refuse, but then he was reaching for her, lifting her up so that she could wrap her legs tightly round him whilst he thrust firmly into her in one long, slow, deliberate movement that made her shudder violently. As he withdrew her muscles tightened, protesting around him, not wanting to let him go, and were then rewarded for their adoration by the almost mind-altering sensation of his second, stronger, deeper thrust. The sensitive nerve-endings in her flesh wept with joy at the intensity. Instinctively Emily drew in her muscles around him, savouring the sensation.

She could feel his hot breath in her ear, the tip of his tongue tracing the curls of flesh. She felt his teeth against the sensitive cord in her neck. Her whole body was being possessed by a pleasure so heightened she thought she might die from it.

'Marco...' She moaned his name as a plea, striking a solitary note of female praise as he thrust deeper, harder and faster now.

'Mmm...more. Marco...more!' she urged him, gasping out aloud in delight as he obeyed her and his movements became fast and rhythmic. Then he drove them to their climaxes, and she was left so boneless and weak that she collapsed helplessly against him, trembling in the aftermath.

The heat of the fury that had driven him was cooling on his sweat-slicked skin. Where he should have felt satisfaction and triumph at making Emily acknowledge that he could still arouse her, Marco could only feel a dark sense of stark awareness that he had crossed over a boundary he should not have breached. In forcing Emily to give in to the desire he had summoned in her, he'd also forced himself to acknowledge his need for her. A fleeting need, brought on by his justifiable anger, he assured himself, that was all! It meant nothing in the broader picture of his life.

'I think we both needed that,' he told her coolly, 'and perhaps it was a fitting end to our relationship, a tribute to the mutual attraction that brought us together.'

Emily couldn't believe what she had done—and what she

might have betrayed. She couldn't bear the thought of Marco thinking now how stupid she had been, maybe guessing she had dreamed that, one day, he might fall in love with her as she had done with him. A wave of irritation surged through her—not against him, but against herself. What a fool she had been, deliberately blinding herself to reality and fixating on something that her common sense could have warned her wouldn't possibly happen. If Marco had really loved her he would have told her so. But he hadn't, and he never would. She had deceived herself just as much as Marco had deceived her, and if anything her crime against herself was even greater than his. The fierce turbulent, almost torrid heat of their love-making had subsided now, and her anger had burned down into stark bleakness and grinding pain. Her dreams had been swept aside, shown to be pitifully worthless. Marco was a stranger to her, but no more so than she felt at this moment she was to herself.

'Mutual attraction then, but perhaps mutual contempt now,' she answered Marco pointedly. 'I'm not the naïve girl that I was when we first became lovers, Marco.'

'Meaning what?' he challenged her, frowning.

'Meaning that I've learned enough about sex from you to know that it isn't always used as an expression of positive emotions. It's common knowledge these days that couples on the verge of splitting up do sometimes use sex as a way of venting their negative feelings. Some couples say that they had the best sex of their relationship when the emotional side of it was dying. Of course, I know that *we* aren't emotionally intimate with one another.' What she meant of course, Emily admitted, was that Marco had never been emotionally close with her, because he didn't want to be, whilst she had had to struggle not to be close when she'd wanted to be. 'But I think both of us would accept that the break-up of any relationship—even one like ours—does bring things to the surface that aren't easy to accept.'

Marco's frown deepened. She was now being far more matter-of-fact about their relationship ending than he had expected—and he didn't like that! But he was being ridiculous. He should feel very relieved that she was being so sensible, especially after her earlier, uncharacteristic outburst…

CHAPTER SIX

FROM his seat on the royal jet, Marco looked down onto his family's private runway at Niroli's airport to where a group of formally dressed courtiers and officials were waiting to greet him. The ostrich-feather plumes of their dress hats fluttered in the breeze as they stood straight-backed, ignoring the heat of the sun. Marco's lips twisted with irony at the thought of the heavily gold-braided, bemedalled uniform that his grandfather had sent him, along with strict instructions that he must wear it when he landed and was greeted by the courtly welcoming committee. In fact, the uniform, appropriate for the rank of Lieutenant Colonel in Niroli's ancient Royal Guard, was lying in its leather dress-trunk in the plane's hold, whilst he wore his own handmade Saville Row suit. His grandfather wouldn't be pleased. But Marco intended to let him, and the court, know right from the word go that he would make his own decisions and judgements and he wouldn't allow them to force theirs on him.

Emily would have appreciated and understood his decision, though she would probably have laughed gently, and teased him as well into wearing that undeniably magnificent, beautifully tailored uniform. Emily...he tried to thrust the thought of her away from him, along with the erotic mental image of her alongside him in his bed that was forming inside his head, but it was too late; she was there, smiling at him, wanting him, as he ached for her. What the hell was this?

He stood up so abruptly that the young Niroli air force aide-de-camp, who'd been sent to escort him home, was caught off guard, and his own attempt to get to his feet before Marco was severely hampered by his ceremonial sword. The red-faced young man saluted as he semi-stuttered, 'Highness, if you wish to have more time in order to prepare, then please allow me—'

'No, I am ready,' Marco told the aide shortly and then relented when he saw his anxious expression. It was not the lad's fault—and he was little more than a boy, a scion of one of Niroli's foremost titled families. Marco had chosen to be the man he was, rather than the grandson his grandfather wanted him to be. Damn Emily for pursuing him like this, insinuating herself into his thoughts where she now had no right to be! Her abrupt departure from his apartment had decided him that he should leave London earlier than he had originally planned—much to his grandfather's delight. Marco suspected the old king would not have been so cock-a-hoop over his 'victory' if he had known that it owed less to his own power than to his grandson's loss of his bed-mate.

The aide-de-camp, who was carrying his own plumed hat as protocol demanded, stood beside his king-to-be as the doors to the royal jet were opened. He bowed as Marco walked past him and stepped out onto the gangway steps and into Niroli's sunshine. Just for a few seconds, Marco stood motionless and ramrod-straight at the top of the steps, not because he was the island's future ruler, but because he was one of its returning sons. He had almost forgotten the unique scent of sunshine and sea, mimosa and lemons, all of which hit him on a surge of hot wind. Not even the strong smell of jet fuel and tarmac could detract from them, and Marco felt emotion sting his eyes: this was his home, his country, and the crowds he could see lining the wide straight road that ran from the airport to the main town were his people. Many of them had not had the benefit of being part of a wider, modern world, but he intended to change that. He would give to Niroli's young the opportunities his grandfather's old-fashioned rule had denied them. Determinedly, Marco stepped forward. The waiting military band broke into Niroli's national anthem and the waiting officials removed their hats and bowed their heads. Their faces were familiar to Marco, although more wrinkled and lined than he remembered—the faces of old men.

As he reached his grandfather's most senior minister the elderly gentleman placed his hands on Marco's arms, greeting him with a traditional continental embrace. His voice shook with emotion and Marco could see that beneath his proud, stern expression and the determinedly upright stance there was a very aged, tired man, who probably would have preferred to spend his last years with his grandchildren than doing his king's bidding. Tactfully, Marco adjusted his own walking pace to that of the courtiers surrounding him as they escorted him unsteadily to the waiting open-topped royal limousine.

At least his grandfather hadn't sent the coronation carriage to collect him, Marco reflected ruefully; its motion was sickeningly rocky and its velvet padded seats unpleasantly hard.

This should be his moment of triumph, the public endorsement of the strength he had gained in becoming his own man. Soon the power of the Royal House of Niroli would become his, and he would step into his grandfather's shoes and fulfil his destiny. So why didn't he feel more excited, and why was there this sense of emptiness within him, this sense of loss, of something missing?

The cavalcade started to move, the waiting crowds began

to cheer, children clutching Niroli flags and leaning dangerously into the road, the better to see him. Marco lifted his hand and began to wave. The cool air-conditioned luxury of the limo protected him from the midday heat. *But what about the people? They must be feeling the heat, Marco.* As clearly as though she were seated at his side, he could hear Emily's gently reproachful voice. Angrily he banished it. The limousine travelled a few more yards and then Marco reached forward, rapping on the glass separating him from the driver and an armed guard.

'Highness?' the guard queried anxiously.

'Stop the car!' Marco ordered. 'I want to get out and walk.' As he reached to open his door the guard looked horrified. 'Sire,' he protested, 'the king…it may not be safe.'

Marco's eyebrow rose. 'Knowing my grandfather as I do, I cannot imagine he has not had ordered that plain-clothes security men be posted amongst the crowd. Besides, these are our people, not our enemy.'

As they saw Marco stepping out of the limousine the crowd fell silent. At no time in living memory had their ruler done anything so informal as walk amongst them. Marco shook the gnarled hands of working men, his smile causing pretty girls to glow with excitement and older women to feel a reawakening frisson of their youths.

One aged woman pushed her way through the people to reach him. Marco could see from her traditional peasant costume that she came from the mountains of Niroli. Her back was bent from long years spent working in the orange groves and vineyards that covered their lower slopes, her face as brown and lined as a wrinkled walnut. But there was still a fiery flash of pride in her dark eyes and as she held out to him the clumsy leather purse she had obviously made herself Marco felt as though a giant hand were gripping his heart in a tight vice.

'Highness, please take this humble gift,' she begged him. 'May it always be kept full, just like the coffers and the nurseries of the House of Niroli.' It was plain that the old peasant could ill afford to give him anything. Indeed, Marco felt he should be the one to give something to her, so he was not surprised to see the angry, hostile glower on the face of the shabbily dressed youth at her side.

'This is your grandson?' Marco asked her as he thanked her for her gift.

'Aye, he is, sire, and he shames me with his sullen looks and lack of appreciation for all that we have here on our island.'

'That is because we have nothing!' the youth burst out angrily, his face now seemingly on fire with emotion. 'We have nothing, whilst others have everything! We come to the town, and we see foreigners with their expensive yachts and their fancy clothes. Our king bends over backwards to welcome them, whilst we mountain-dwellers do not even have electricity. They look at us as though we are nothing, and that is because, to our king, we *are* nothing!'

Suddenly, like a cloud passing over the sun, the mood of the crowd gathered around Marco had changed. He could see the anger in the faces of the group of rough-looking, poorly dressed young men who had joined the outspoken youth. The first of his grandfather's security guards rushed to protect Marco, but very firmly he stepped between them, saying clearly, 'It is good to know that the people of Niroli are able to speak their minds freely to me. This issue of getting electricity to the more remote parts of our island is one that has, I know, taxed His Majesty's thoughts for a long time.' Marco put his hand on the angry youth's shoulder, drawing him closer to him, whilst he gave the hovering guards a small dismissive shake of his head. He could see the grateful tears in the old peasant woman's eyes.

'My grandson speaks without thinking,' she told him huskily. 'But, at heart, he is a good boy and as devoted to the king as anyone.'

The youth's friends were hurrying him away and Marco allowed himself to be escorted back to his limo. Once inside, he realised that he was still holding the old woman's carefully made purse. There was anger in his heart now, pressing down on him like an unwanted heavy weight. Niroli's royal family was the richest in the world and yet some of its subjects were living lives of utmost poverty. He could well imagine how upset and shocked Emily would have been if she had witnessed what had just happened. The leather purse felt soft and warm to his touch. He was the one who should be giving to his people, not the other way around. His time away from the island had changed him more than he had realised, Marco acknowledged, and somehow he didn't think his grandfather was going to like what he had in mind...

Huddled into an armchair in the sitting room of her small Chelsea house, a prettily embroidered throw wrapped around her like a comfort blanket, Emily let the full rip-tide of her anguish take her over. What was the point in trying to fight it or escape it? The reality was that Marco, no, *Prince Marco, soon to be King Marco*, she corrected herself miserably, had gone, not just from her life, but from Britain itself, to return to his home, his throne and his people. Ultimately her place in his life would be filled by someone else. She gave a small low cry as more pain seized her, and then reminded herself angrily that the man she loved did not exist; he had been a creation of her own imagination and his deceit. Everything they had shared had been based on lies; every time he had held her or touched her she had been giving the whole of herself to him, whilst he had been withholding virtually everything of his true self. But even knowing this, as the numbing shock of her discovery of the truth rose and retreated, she was left with the agonising reality that she still loved him.

As much as she despised herself for not being able to cease wanting him, because she knew just how much he had deceived her, her self-contempt could not drive out her love.

What was he doing now? Was he thinking at all of her? Missing her? *Stop it, stop it,* all her inner protective instincts demanded in agony. She must not do this to herself! She must accept that he had gone, and that she had to find a way of living without him and the comfort of being able to look back and know that they had shared something very special. It was over, they were over, and her pride was demanding that she accept that and get on with her life. She was as much a fool for letting him into her thoughts now as she had been for letting him into her life. There was one thing for sure: he would not be thinking about her. He would not have given her a single thought since she had walked out of his apartment, following that dreadful discovery and the bitterly corrosive row that had ended their relationship

What a total fool she had been for deluding herself into thinking that he would ever return her love…

CHAPTER SEVEN

'So, Marco, what is this that the Chief of Police tells me about your welcome parade? About your being threatened by some wretched insurrectionist from the mountains? Probably one of the Viallis. Mind you, you have only yourself to blame. Had you not taken it into your head to so rashly get out of the car, it would not have happened. You must remember that you are my heir and Niroli's next king. It is not wise to court danger.'

'There wasn't any real danger. The boy—for he was little more than that—was simply voicing—'

'His hostility to the throne!' King Giorgio interrupted Marco angrily.

His grandfather had aged since he had last seen him, but the old patriarch still had about him an awesome aura of power, Marco admitted ruefully. The problem was that it no longer particularly impressed Marco—he had power of his own now, power that came from living his life in his own way. He knew that his grandfather sensed this in him and that it irked him. That was why he insisted on taking his grandson to task over the incident at his welcoming parade.

'My feeling was that the boy was more frustrated and resentful than hostile.'

Marco watched his grandfather. There was a larger issue at

stake here than the boy's angry words, one which Marco felt was essential, but which he knew wasn't something his grandfather would be happy to discuss.

Nevertheless, Marco had been doing some investigation of his own, and what he had discovered had highlighted potential problems within Niroli that needed addressing before they developed into much more worrying conflicts.

'The boy was complaining about the lack of an electricity supply to his village. He resents the fact that visitors to our country have benefits that some of our own people do not.' Marco held his ground as his grandfather's fist came crashing down on the desk between them.

'I will not listen to this foolish nonsense. Tourists bring money into the country and, naturally, we have to lure them here by providing them with the kind of facilities they are used to.'

'Whilst some amongst our people go without them?' Marco challenged him coolly. 'Angry young men do sometimes behave rashly. But surely it is our duty to equip our subjects with what they need to move into the twenty-first century? Our schoolchildren cannot learn properly without access to computers, and if we deprive them of the ability to do so then we will be maintaining an underclass within the heart of our country.'

'You dare to lecture me on how to rule?' the king bellowed. 'You, who turned your back on Niroli to live a life of your own choosing in London?'

'You're the one who has summoned me back, Nonno,' Marco reminded him, lowering his voice and deliberately using his childhood pet name for his grandfather in an attempt to soften the old man's mood. It was easy sometimes to forget his grandfather was ninety, yet still immoveable about what the right thing was for Niroli and its people. Marco didn't want to upset the king too much.

'Because I had no other choice,' Giorgio growled. 'You are my direct heir, Marco, for all that you choose to behave like a commoner, rather than a member of the ruling House of Niroli. At least you had the sense to leave that…that floozy you were living with behind when you returned home.'

Anger flashed in Marco's eyes. It was typical of his grandfather to have found out as much about his private life in London as he could. It also infuriated him that Giorgio should refer to Emily in that way and dismiss their relationship. Worse, it felt as though, somehow, his grandfather had touched a raw place within him that he didn't want to admit existed, never mind be reminded about. Because, even though he didn't want to own up to it, he was missing Emily. Marco shrugged the thought aside. So what if he was? Wasn't it only natural that his body, deprived of the sexual pleasure it had shared with hers, should ache a little?

'As to what we agreed, it was simply that I should *initially* return to Niroli alone,' Marco pointed out.

Immediately the king's anger returned. 'What do you mean, "initially"?'

When Marco didn't answer him, the old man bellowed, 'You will not bring her here, Marco! I will not allow it. You are my heir, and you have a position to maintain. The people—'

Marco knew that he should reassure his grandfather and tell him he had no intention of bringing Emily to Niroli, but instead he said coolly, 'The people, our people, will, I am sure, have more important things to worry about than the fact that I have a mistress—things like the fact that ten per cent of them do not have electricity.'

'You are trying to meddle in things that are not your concern,' the king told him sharply. 'Take care, Marco, otherwise, you will have people thinking that you are more fitted to be a dissident than a leader. To rule, you must command respect and in order to do that you must show a strong hand. The people are your children and need to look up to you as their father, as someone wiser than them.'

This was an issue on which he and his grandfather would never see eye to eye, Marco knew…

'Emily, why don't you call it a day and go home? No one else will come into the shop now and you don't have any more client appointments. I know you hate me keeping on about this, but you really don't look at all well. I can lock up the premises for you.'

Emily forced herself to give her assistant an I'm-all-right smile. Jemma wasn't wrong, though she didn't like the fact that the girl had noticed how unwell she looked, because she didn't want to have to answer questions about the cause. 'It's kind of you to offer to do that, Jemma,' she answered, 'but…'

'But you're missing Marco desperately, and you don't want to go back to an empty house?' Jemma suggested gently, her words slicing through the barriers Emily had tried so desperately to maintain.

She could feel betraying tears burning the backs of her eyes. She had tried so very hard to pretend that she didn't mind that she and Marco had split up, but it was obvious that her assistant hadn't been deceived.

'It had to end, given Marco's royal status,' she told Jemma, trying to keep her voice light. Initially, she had worried about revealing the truth of Marco's real identity. But, in the end, she'd had no need to do so because her assistant had seen one of many articles appearing in the press about Marco's return to Niroli; most of them had been accompanied by photographs of his cavalcade and the crowd waiting to welcome him. 'I just wish that he had told me the truth about himself, Jemma,' Emily said in a low voice, unable to conceal her hurt.

'I can understand that,' Jemma agreed. 'But according to what I've read, Marco came over here incognito because he wanted to prove himself in his own right. He had already done that by the time he met you, yet I suppose he could hardly tell you his real identity—not only would it have been difficult for him to just turn round and say, "Oh, by the way, perhaps I ought to tell you that I'm a prince," he most probably wanted you to value him for himself, not for his title or position.'

Emily could see the logic of Jemma's argument, and she knew it was one that Marco himself would have used—had they ever got to the stage of discussing the issue.

'Marco didn't tell me because he *didn't want* to tell me,' she retorted, trying to harden her heart against its betraying softening. 'To him, I was just a…a…temporary bed-mate—a diversion he could enjoy, before he left me to get on with the really serious business of his life and return to Niroli.'

'I think I know how you must be feeling,' Jemma allowed, 'but I did read in one article that it wasn't until the death of his parents in an accident that Marco became the next in line to the throne. I'm sure he didn't tell you because he assumed he would continue to live in London with you anonymously.'

'I meant nothing to him.'

'I can't believe that, Emily. You always seemed so happy together, and so well suited.'

'It's pointless talking about it, or him, now. It's over.'

'Is it? I can't help thinking that there's a lot of unfinished business between the two of you,' Jemma told her softly. 'I know from what you told me that you left the apartment virtually as soon as you discovered the truth. You must have still been in shock when that happened, and my guess is that Marco must have been equally shocked, although for different reasons.'

'Reasons like being found out, you mean, and resenting me being the one to end our relationship, not him?' Emily asked her bitterly.

'So, you wouldn't be interested if he got in touch with you?' Jemma probed quietly.

'That isn't going to happen.' But she knew from the look in her assistant's eyes that Jemma had guessed her weakness and how much a foolish, treacherous part of her still longed for him.

'Be fair to yourself, Emily,' Jemma told her. 'You and Marco have history together, and there are still loose ends for you that need proper closure, questions you need to ask and answers Marco needs to give you. A poisoned wound can't heal,' she pointed out wisely. 'And until you get that poison of your break-up out of your system, you won't heal.'

'I'm fine,' Emily lied defensively.

'No, you aren't,' Jemma responded firmly. 'Just look at yourself. You aren't eating, you're losing weight and you obviously aren't happy.'

'It's just this virus, that's all. I can't seem to throw it off properly,' Emily told her. But she knew that Jemma wasn't deceived.

Emily was still thinking about her conversation with Jemma more than two hours later as she wandered aimlessly round her showroom, pausing to straighten a line of already perfectly straight sample swatches. Jemma had been right about her not wanting to return to her empty house and correct too about how much she was missing Marco.

It had been all very well telling herself that he had lied to her and that she was better off without him. The reality was very different: the empty space he'd left in her life had been taken over by the unending misery of living without him. He had only been gone just a short time, but already she had lost

count of the number of times every night she woke up
reaching out for him in her bed, only to be filled with anguish
when the reality that he wasn't there hit her once more. No
matter how hard she worked, she couldn't fill her mind with
enough things to block out the knowledge that Marco had left;
that she wouldn't be going home to him; that never again
would he hold her, or touch her, or kiss her; never ever again.
It was over, and somehow she must find a way to rebuild her
life, although right now she had no idea how she was going
to accomplish that. To make matters worse, as Jemma had
already commented, she was losing weight and felt unable to
eat properly. Emily had put it down to a flu bug she had picked
up earlier in the year. She just couldn't seem to get rid of it.

Allied to which, she had an even nastier heartache bug,
Emily recognised. Did Marco think of her at all, now he was
living his new life, Emily wondered miserably, or was he far
too busy planning his future? A future that was ultimately, and
surely, bound to include a wife. Pain seized her, ripping at her
all her defences, leaving her exposed to the reality of what
loving him really meant. Marco…Marco… How could this
have happened to her? How could she have avoided falling in
love with him? What was he doing right now? Who was he
with? His grandfather? His family? She mustn't do this to
herself, Emily warned herself tiredly. It served no purpose,
other than to reinforce what she already knew, and that was
that she loved a man who did not love her. She reached for her
coat. She might as well go home.

'What is this I hear about you returning to London? I will not
allow you to leave Niroli to go to London. What possible
reason could you have for wanting to be there?'

Marco had to struggle to stop himself from responding in
kind to his grandfather's angry interrogation.

'You know why I need to return. I have certain business matters to attend to there,' he answered suavely instead.

'I do not permit it.'

'No? That is your choice, Grandfather, but I still intend to go. You see, I do not need your permission.'

Obstinately they eyed each other, two alpha males who knew that, according to the law of the jungle, only one of them could truly hold the reins of power. Marco had no intention of allowing his grandfather to dominate him. He knew well enough that once he let him have the upper hand, the king would treat him with contempt. Giorgio was the kind of man who would rather die with his sword in his hand, so to speak, than allow a younger rival to take it from him. The truth was that Marco could have dealt with the business that was taking him to the UK from the island, and that, in part, his decision to go to London in spite of his grandfather's objections had been made publicly to underline his own determination and status. It was more than two weeks since he had first arrived on Niroli, and there hadn't been a single day when he and his grandfather hadn't clashed like two Titans. Every attempt he had made to talk to Giorgio about doing something to help the poorer inhabitants of the island had been met with a furious tirade about what a waste of money this would be, and a threat to royal rule.

Marco was determined that electricity should be made available to those living in the more remote villages, and his grandfather was equally adamant that he was not prepared to sanction it.

'Very well, then, I shall pay for it myself,' Marco had told him grimly. But the reality was that things were not as simple as that: the topography of the mountain region meant that they would need to bring in expert outside help, and it was of course Vialli country.

Marco suspected that King Giorgio was being difficult for the sake of being difficult, more than anything else. He could also admit to himself that his years in London running his own life and not having to worry about consulting anyone about his decisions was now making it very difficult for him to conform to the role of king-in-waiting. He was very much the junior partner in this new relationship. He started to walk away.

'Marco, I trust that this visit of yours to London does not have anything to do with that woman you were bedding?'

Marco swung round and looked at his grandfather, his voice flattened by the weight of his fury as he demanded, 'And if it does?'

'Then I forbid you to see her,' his grandfather told him fiercely. 'The future King of Niroli does not bed some commoner—a divorcée, with no pedigree and no money.'

'No one tells me who I can and cannot take to my bed, Grandfather, not even you.' Marco didn't wait to hear what the older man might say in reply. Instead he strode out of the room, fighting to dampen down the heat of the fury burning along his veins. The bright sunshine that had warmed the air earlier that day was turning to vivid dusk as he left the palace. He had refused the offer of a suite of rooms within its walls, preferring instead to stay in the nearby villa he had inherited from his parents. His grandfather hadn't been too pleased about that, but Marco had refused to give in. It was very important to him that he retained his privacy and independence. However, right now, it wasn't the villa he was heading for as he climbed into his personal car. He was bound for the airport, and a flight to London, despite his grandfather's opposition. How dared Giorgio attempt to tell him that he couldn't sleep with Emily? He glanced at the clock on the dashboard of his car. It would be early evening in London, just after six o'clock. Emily would most probably have left her shop and be on her way home.

Emily! It hadn't needed his grandfather's mention of her to bring her into his thoughts. Indeed, it had surprised and disconcerted him to discover just how much she had been there since they had parted. It was only because he was discovering that he wasn't enjoying sleeping alone, he assured himself. The fact that Emily was so constantly in his thoughts was simply his mind playing tricks and had no personal relevance for him.

He turned his thoughts back to his grandfather; despite his frustration with the older man's arrogant and domineering attitude, he was very aware that the king was not in the best of health. He must continue to temper his reaction to him as much as he could. But it wasn't easy.

'Emily, why don't you go and see your doctor?' Jemma suggested, her face shadowed with concern as she studied Emily's wan complexion.

'There's no need for that. It's as I've said before—it's just that virus hanging around,' Emily explained tiredly. 'The doctor will only tell me to take some paracetamol, and that it's bound to wear off soon.'

'You've been sick every morning this week, and now you've left your lunch. You look exhausted.'

'I need a holiday, some sunshine to perk me up a bit, that's all,' Emily replied lightly. She didn't want to continue this discussion, but she didn't want to hurt Jemma's feelings either; she knew her assistant was genuinely concerned about her.

'You certainly need something—or someone,' Jemma agreed forthrightly, leaving Emily regretting that she had ever allowed her guard to slip and admit that she was missing Marco.

'Why don't I pop across the road and bring you back a sandwich and a cup of coffee?' Jemma suggested.

'Coffee?' Emily shuddered with revulsion. The very

thought made her feel nauseous. 'I couldn't face it,' she protested. 'Just thinking about the smell makes me feel sick.'

'I think you're right about you needing a holiday,' Jemma told her firmly.

Emily gave her a forced smile. The truth was, what she needed and wanted more than anything else was Marco—Marco's arms—to hold her close, Marco's body next to hers in bed at night and, most of all, Marco's love, and the knowledge that it would last a lifetime. But she wasn't going to be given any of those. She hadn't realised just how hard it would be for her after their relationship had ended. The emotional pain she was suffering now was almost unendurable; it tore through her emotions like a fever in her blood, burning up her immunity. Every night when she went to bed she told herself that it couldn't get any worse and that soon she would start to feel better. But every morning when she woke up it *was* worse. She hated herself for wanting him like this after the way he had deceived her. However, hating herself couldn't stop her from loving him...

The business that had brought Marco to London had been concluded, and the first consignment of the generators he'd bought at his own expense were already on their way to the airport to be flown out by a cargo plane to Niroli. He had been on his way back to his hotel when, for no logical reason he could find, he had leaned forward and told the cab driver he had changed his mind, then given him the address of Emily's small shop in Chelsea. He didn't owe her anything; she had refused to let him fully explain to her that his decision to conceal his real identity had been one he had made long before he had met her. Sleeping dogs were best left to lie and, anyway, their relationship would have had to end sooner or later.

Marco's purchase of the generators would infuriate his

grandfather, as would the knowledge that he was seeing Emily, he acknowledged as he paid the cab fare and looked along the pretty Chelsea street basking in afternoon sunshine. So was that why he was here? To infuriate his grandfather? Marco's mouth curled in sardonic awareness. The days when he had been immature enough to need to infuriate the man he had seen as an unwanted authority figure were long gone. No, he didn't want to upset his grandfather at all. But he was not quite ready to let go or move on. Therefore a little reinforcement to him of the fact that Marco wasn't going to be dictated to wouldn't do any harm. Plus, he liked the idea of dealing with two separate issues at a single stroke—Emily had walked out on him without giving him the chance to explain his situation to her rationally. She owed him that opportunity and his pride demanded that she retract the contemptuously angry insults she had thrown at him. That was what had brought him here: his own pride. And no one, not his grandfather, and certainly not Emily herself, was going to stop him from seeing her and demanding that his pride was satisfied. And his body, which needed satisfaction so desperately? Any woman could provide him with that! Marco dismissed the throb that was increasing with every step that took him closer to Emily. No way would he ever allow one woman to dominate his senses to that extent.

He could see into the window of her shop-cum-showroom from where he was standing. The simple elegance of the set Emily had created was both immediately refreshing and soothing on his eye. She had a remarkable, indeed an inspired, gift for transforming the dull and utilitarian. His Niroli villa could certainly do with her skills!

Marco began to frown. Whilst he had to admit how poorly the décor of his villa compared with that of the London apartment Emily had decorated for him, he could well imagine his grandfather's reaction if he were to return to the island with her at his side, claiming that he needed an interior designer. His grandfather wouldn't believe him for one moment and he would think that Marco was deliberately flouting his orders. Perhaps he should flout them in this way, Marco reflected ruefully; it would be a sure and certain way of making his grandfather understand that he wasn't going to be pushed around. And Emily's presence on Niroli and in his life wouldn't directly impact on their subjects.

The more he thought about it, the more Marco could see the benefit to himself of Emily's temporary and brief presence on the island as a sharp warning to his grandfather not to trespass into his privacy. Certainly in the unlikely event of Emily being willing to return to Niroli with him, he would want her to share his bed. He would be a fool not to, given the level of his current sexual hunger. Was that really why he was here now? Not solely because of his pride, but because he still wanted her too?

No!

He was already pushing open the shop door, but then he paused, half inclined to turn round and walk away just to prove how unfounded that motivation was. However, it was too late for him to change his mind: Emily had seen him.

She was sitting behind a desk talking with her assistant, Jemma, and the first thing Marco noticed was how much weight she had lost and how pale and fragile she looked. Because of him? It shocked him to discover that a part of him wanted to believe it was because she was missing him. Why? *Why* should he feel like this when, in the past, with other women, he had been only too pleased to see them move on to a new partner after he had broken up with them. But in the past he hadn't continued to want those other women, had he?

He pushed his thoughts to one side, watching Emily's eyes widen as she looked up and saw him, the blood rushing to her face, turning it a deep pink. He saw her lips frame his name. She pushed back her chair to stand up and then he saw her sway and start to crumple, as though her body were no more than one of the swathes of fabric draped over the back of another chair nearby. That deep pink glow had receded from her cheeks, leaving her so pale that she looked almost bloodless.

He reacted immediately and instinctively, pushing his way through the pieces of furniture, reaching her just in time to hear her saying huskily, 'It's all right, I'm not going to faint,' before she did exactly that.

Through the roaring blur of sick dizziness, Emily could hear voices: Jemma's sharp with anxiety, Marco's harsher than she wanted it to be, their words, moving giddily in and out of one another, weaving through the darkness she was trying to free herself from. Then she felt Marco's arms tightening around her, holding her, and she exhaled on a small sigh of relief, knowing she was safe and that she didn't have to battle on alone any more. Gratefully she let the darkness take her as she slid into a faint.

'What the hell's going on?' Marco asked Jemma abruptly. Any idiotic thought he might have entertained that there was something ego-boosting about Emily's reaction to him had disappeared now, banished by his realisation of just how fragile she was. In all the time they had been together he had never once known her faint, or even say that she thought she might be going to, which made it all the more shocking that she had done so now.

'I wish I knew,' Jemma admitted. 'What I do know is that she hasn't been eating properly. She says it's because of that flu bug she had earlier in the year. She just can't seem to throw it off. She isn't the only one, of course. I read in a newspaper the other day that many people are still suffering from its after-effects. The health authorities say that the best cures are rest and sunshine to build up the immune system. Emily's admitted as much herself, although I can't see her taking a holiday. I'm so glad you're here. I've been really worried about her.'

'Will you both please stop talking about me as though I don't exist? I'm all right…' The blackness was receding and with it her nausea. She was sitting on a chair—Marco must have put her there, and no doubt he was the one who had pushed her head down towards her knees as well. She turned her head slightly and saw that he was standing next to her. So close to her, in fact, that she could easily have reached out and touched him. Weak tears stung her eyes, causing her to make a small anguished sound of protest.

'Emily?' She could feel Marco's hand on her shoulder, her flesh responding to its familiar warmth, weirdly both soothed and excited by it. The hardness of his voice lacerated both her pride and her heart. This was not how she would have wanted them to meet for the first time after their split; she must seem so vulnerable and needy, virtually forcing Marco to step in and manage things. Fate wasn't being very kind to her at the moment, she reflected wearily. She held her breath as Marco crouched down beside her, struggling to lift her head and fight off the swimming sensation within it. She would have given a lot for him not to have seen her like this, not to have witnessed her humiliating loss of consciousness.

'There's no need to fuss. I'm fine,' she repeated, sounding as steady as she could.

'Don't listen to her, Marco. She isn't all right at all. She's hardly eating and when she does, she's sick.'

'Jemma!' Emily warned sharply.

'Jemma is hardly breaking the Official Secrets Act,' Marco defended her assistant dryly. 'After all, she hasn't told me anything I can't see for myself. And, besides, there's no reason why I shouldn't know, is there?'

None, except her pride and her aching heart, Emily admitted inwardly. And, of course, those wouldn't matter to Marco. 'I don't know what you are doing here, *Your Highness*,' she addressed him, deliberately underlining his title.

He couldn't just walk away and leave her like this, Marco decided. So what was he going to do? His return flight was already scheduled for later this evening. Emily wasn't his responsibility. She was an adult. There was no good cause for him to involve himself here. But another voice deep inside him told him it was too late for such arguments. He had already made his decision.

'I came to see you because I've got a business proposition to put to you,' he told Emily levelly. He could see her eyes widening with confusion and disbelief. She was lifting her hand to her head, as though she couldn't take in what he was saying. Seeing her look so thin and unwell touched an unfamiliar chord inside him, which he crushed down the instant he felt it.

Emily's head was aching painfully. She was finding it hard enough to grasp that Marco was actually here, never mind anything else. Her thoughts were in complete disarray. She couldn't really comprehend what he was saying. It was difficult enough for her to focus simply on stopping her heart from spinning and shaking her body with the force of its frantic beats, without having to think logically and calmly as well. It had upset her far more than she wanted to admit that the sight of him should have affected her to such an extent that she had collapsed. Worryingly, even now her senses were still clinging possessively to the memory of being held in his arms as he had caught her. Part of her, the sensible part, she told herself firmly, wanted to put as much distance between them as she could, to protect herself from making it even more obvious just how intensely aware of him she was. Whilst the other part longed to be as intimately close to him as it was possible to be: body to body, skin to skin, mouth to mouth—heart to heart.

'A business proposition?' she repeated uncertainly. 'What exactly does that mean, Marco? I'm an interior designer.'

'Exactly,' Marco agreed, 'and a very good one.'

Marco was praising her? *Flattering her?* Why? she wondered suspiciously. It was totally out of character for him to behave like this.

'Since it could be a while before I formally take over from my grandfather, instead of moving into the palace and being cooped up in a suite of rooms there,' Marco told her, 'I've moved into a villa I inherited from my parents. It's in the old part of the town and it's badly in need of modernisation. I want a designer who knows what she's doing and, just as important, one who knows my taste.'

It took several seconds for the full meaning of what he was saying to sink in. But once it had, Emily could hardly conceal her disbelief.

'Are you saying that you want to commission *me* to be that designer?' she asked Marco faintly.

'Yes, why not?' Marco confirmed.

'Why not?' Emily stared at him, as her heart lurched crazily into her ribs. 'Marco, we were lovers, and now our relationship is over. You must see that I can't just let you commission me as your designer as though everything that took place between us never happened.'

'Of course not, Emily. You never let me explain properly to you why I didn't tell you about Niroli or my role there.' Out of the corner of her eye, Emily could see Jemma discreetly edging out of the room to go into the stock room, closing the door after her to give them some privacy.

Emily waited, feeling helpless and weak. She was her own worst enemy, she knew that. She shouldn't even be thinking of listening to him, instead of sitting here desperate for every second she could spend with him.

'As a boy, I had a very difficult relationship with my grandfather. I suppose I was something of a black sheep in his eyes. I resented the way he treated my father, who was too gentle to stand up to him, and I swore that I would never let him control me the way he did my parents. I came to London determined to prove to him and to myself that I could be a success without the power of the Royal House of Niroli. It was for that reason that I came here and stayed incognito, and no other.'

'But when we met, you had achieved that success, Marco,' Emily forced herself to remind him.

'Yes, but I had also grown used to the freedom of living and proving myself as plain Marco Fierezza. It seemed to me then that there was no need for me to live any other way—at least not for many years. My father was still alive and he would have succeeded my grandfather when the time came.' Marco gave a small shrug. 'I had no expectation of becoming king until I was much older.'

'Maybe not. But you would surely have to marry appropriately and produce a son to whom you can pass on the crown,' Emily couldn't help pointing out quietly.

Marco inclined his head.

'Yes, at some stage. One of the archaic rules that surround the Royal House of Niroli is that the king cannot marry a woman who is divorced, or of ill repute. The challenge of finding such a paragon in today's world is such that I was more than happy to remain unmarried until necessity directed otherwise.'

Emily had to blink fast to disperse her threatening tears. Marco obviously had no idea just how hurtful his casual words were. It could never have occurred to him to think of her as someone he might love and want to commit to permanently. She should hate him for showing her how indifferent he was to her, Emily told herself, but somehow she felt too sick at heart to do it.

'Look,' Marco told her crisply, 'I don't have much time, and since you obviously need to eat, why don't we discuss this over an early dinner?'

Emily shuddered and shook her head in instant denial, her reaction making him frown. She'd always had a good appetite, having never needed to worry about what she ate. But now the fact that she had not been eating properly was plain to see in the sharp angles of her cheek-bones and her jaw.

'Jemma's right, Emily, you aren't looking after yourself properly,' Marco announced firmly. 'You need a break. I don't have time to argue with you. I've made up my mind. You're coming back to Niroli with me.'

Was this giddy, soaring feeling inside her really because she was so weak that she was glad that Marco had made up her mind for her? She was an independent woman, for heaven's sake, not some wilting Victorian heroine. She tried to wrench back some control of what was happening.

'I can't do that, Marco. For one thing, there's the business—'

'Of course you can, Em. I can take care of things here,' Jemma piped up from the threshold of the storeroom. With Niroli's back to her, she mouthed to Emily, Go with him, you know you want to… Before announcing to both of them that time was getting on and she had to catch the post with some invoices.

Emily and Marco were alone in the shop now, and she wished violently that she were not so all-consumingly aware of him.

'You can't take me back with you, Marco. It wouldn't work. We were lovers—'

'And still could be, if that's what you want,' Marco interrupted softly.

Emily didn't dare look at him in case he saw the hope and the longing in her eyes. She struggled between her own helpless awareness of how much she still wanted him and the practicalities of the situation, protesting unsteadily, 'Marco, we can't. Even if I wanted to…to go back, it isn't possible.'

'Why not, if it's what both of us want?'

What *both* of them wanted. Her heart lurched, joyously intoxicated by the pleasure of hearing the admission his words contained.

'But what about the rules of the House of Niroli? Surely your grandfather wouldn't approve, or—'

'My grandfather doesn't rule my personal life,' Marco responded with familiar arrogance.

She had no idea how to handle this. She shook her head. 'I don't know what to say,' she admitted. 'How long have I got?'

'To share my bed?' Marco cut her off smoothly. 'I doubt that my grandfather is really ready to step down, for all that he says he is. We could have the summer together and then reassess the situation.'

Emily could feel her face burning.

'That wasn't what I meant. When I said how long have I got, I meant how much time will you give me to think things through before I make up my mind about your business proposition?' she told him primly. 'Nothing else.'

'No time. Because you aren't going to think about it. You are coming back with me, Emily—you don't have a choice about that. What you can choose, though, of course, is in what capacity. My flight leaves at eight, so we've just got time to go back to your house and collect your passport, and anything else you might need. And time for me to show you exactly what both of us will be missing if you don't,' he told

The Harlequin Reader Service® — Here's how it works:

Accepting your 2 free books and 2 free mystery gifts places you under no obligation to buy anything. You may keep the books and gifts and return the shipping statement marked "cancel". If you do not cancel, about a month later we'll send you 6 additional books and bill you just $3.80 each in the U.S. or $4.47 each in Canada, plus 25¢ shipping & handling per book and applicable taxes if any.* That's the complete price and — compared to cover prices of $4.50 each in the U.S. and $5.25 each in Canada — it's quite a bargain! You may cancel at any time, but if you choose to continue, every month we'll send you 6 more books, which you may either purchase at the discount price or return to us and cancel your subscription.

*Terms and prices subject to change without notice. Sales tax applicable in N.Y. Canadian residents will be charged applicable provincial taxes and GST. All orders subject to approval. Credit or debit balances in a customer's account(s) may be offset by any other outstanding balance owed by or to the customer. Please allow 4 to 6 weeks for delivery.

GET FREE BOOKS and FREE GIFTS WHEN YOU PLAY THE...

Lucky 7

SLOT MACHINE GAME!

Just scratch off the silver box with a coin. Then check below to see the gifts you get!

YES! I have scratched off the silver box. Please send me the 2 free Harlequin Presents® books and 2 free gifts for which I qualify. I understand I am under no obligation to purchase any books, as explained on the back of this card.

306 HDL ELUX   **106 HDL EL2M**

FIRST NAME	LAST NAME

ADDRESS

APT.#	CITY

STATE/PROV.	ZIP/POSTAL CODE

7 7 7	Worth TWO FREE BOOKS plus 2 BONUS Mystery Gifts!
🍒 🍒 🍒	Worth TWO FREE BOOKS!
♣ ♣ ♣	Worth ONE FREE BOOK!
🔔 🔔 🍒	TRY AGAIN!

www.eHarlequin.com

(H-HP-07/07)

Offer limited to one per household and not valid to current Harlequin Presents® subscribers.

Your Privacy - Harlequin Books is committed to protecting your privacy. Our Privacy Policy is available online at www.eHarlequin.com or upon request from the Harlequin Reader Service. From time to time we make our lists of customers available to reputable firms who may have a product or service of interest to you. If you would prefer for us not to share her, giving her a look that was so explicitly sexual that her whole body burned with longing. And then, as though he had said nothing remotely outrageous to her, he continued smoothly, 'I should warn you, the villa is going to tax even your creative eye, but I'm sure you'll enjoy the challenge.'

He was handing her her handbag and her coat, and somehow or other she was being ushered out of the door, helpless to stop what was happening and not really caring that she couldn't.

'How many bedrooms does the villa have?' she managed to ask Marco slightly breathlessly, once they were outside on the street.

The look he gave her as he turned to her made her heart thud recklessly.

'Five, but you will be sleeping in mine—with me.'

'You're going to be Niroli's next king, Marco!' Emily felt bound to remind him. 'You can't live openly with me there as your mistress.'

'No?' he challenged her softly.

CHAPTER EIGHT

AT SOME stage during the drive from Niroli's airport, into which they had flown by private jet, she must have half fallen asleep, Emily realised as the motion of the car ceased and she heard Marco's voice saying through the darkness of the car's interior, 'We're here.'

But not before she had seen the impressively straight road leading from the airport, with huge placards attached to lamp-posts bearing a photograph of Marco, a royal crown hovering several centimetres above his head and an ermine-edged cape around his shoulders. Underneath were Italian words, which she could just about translate as, 'Welcome home, Your Highness'.

It made her shiver slightly now to think about them and to remember how she had felt at seeing them, how very aware they had made her of the gulf between her and Marco's royal status.

The emotional roller-coaster ride of the last few hours had taken its toll on her, Emily knew. It had drained her and left her feeling so exhausted that she barely had the energy to get out of the car, even though Marco opened the door for her and reached out his hand to support her. Just for a moment she hesitated and looked back into the car. Wishing she had not come? She pushed the thought aside and focused instead on the fact that the night air had that familiar scent of

Mediterranean warmth that she remembered from her many holidays elsewhere in the region with Marco: a.mingling of olfactory textures and tints, ripened by the day's sunlight and then distilled by the soft darkness.

Emily breathed it in slowly, trying to steady her own nerves. She was, she realised, standing in the courtyard of what looked like a haphazard jumble of white stone walls, shuttered, arched windows and delicate iron balconies, illuminated by moonlight and lamplight from the surrounding buildings. The courtyard was shielded from the narrow street outside by a pair of heavy wooden doors, and as Emily's senses adjusted themselves to the darkness she could hear from somewhere the sound of water from a fountain falling into a basin.

'It looks almost Moorish,' she told Marco.

'Yes, it does, doesn't it?' Marco agreed with her. 'History does have it that the Moors *were* here at one time, and it's here in the oldest part of the main town that you can see their architectural influence. Although there were also Nirolians who travelled as traders to and from Andalucia in Spain, as well.' He was guiding her towards an impressive doorway as he spoke. Emily hesitated, knowing it was too late now to change her mind about the wisdom of allowing him to bring her here and yet not totally able to overcome her uncertainty.

'You said that you're living here, instead of at the palace?'

'Yes. Are you disappointed? If so, I am sure I can arrange for us to have a suite of rooms there—'

Us? 'No…' Emily stopped him hurriedly. 'Marco…' She stopped, and shivered slightly despite the warmth of the air. She was a fool to have allowed Marco to steamroller her into coming here so that he could have her back in his bed, when she knew there was no real future for her with him. But why think of the future when she could have the present? an inner voice urged her. Every day she could have with Marco, every hour, were things so precious she should reach out and grab them with both hands. Emily squeezed her eyes tightly closed and then opened them again. She wasn't used to this unfamiliar recklessness she seemed to have developed, with its blinkered refusal to acknowledge any-thing other than her determination to be with him. She did love him so much, Emily accepted, but it would be far better for her if she did not.

Fine, the reckless voice told her. *So you spend your time trying to stop loving him, and I'll spend mine enjoying being with him. You can't leave—not now.* What *was* this? She felt as though she were being torn in two. The sensible, protective part of her was telling her that it would be better if she spent her time here learning to recognise the huge differences between them; far better if she made herself focus, not on the fact that Marco was her lover and the man she loved, but on the fact that he was Niroli's future king and as such could never be hers. However, this new reckless part of her was insisting that nothing mattered more than squeezing the intimacy and the sweetness out of every extra minute she had with him, regardless of what the future might bring. How could she bring together two such opposing forces? She couldn't.

'Let's go inside,' she heard Marco telling her, 'then I can introduce you to Maria and Pietro who look after the villa for me.'

Emily still hung back.

'They are bound to talk about my being here.'

'I expect they will, but why should that matter?' Marco knew all too well that they would, and that their talk would very quickly reach his grandfather's ears. There was no need for him to share that knowledge with Emily, though.

'Wouldn't it perhaps be better if…well, you said you wanted me to restyle the villa. Perhaps I should have my own room, for convention's sake, and then you could…'

'I could what? Sneak you into my bed at dead of night?' Marco shook his head, his mouth tightening. 'I am a man, Emily, not a fearful boy.'

'But if we are going to be lovers…'

'"If" we are?' he mocked her softly. 'There is no "if" about it, Emily. You will be sleeping in my bed and I shall be there with you, make no mistake about that. I know you're tired, so I shall not make love to you, but only for tonight. My people will understand that I am a man, as well as their future king, and they will not expect me to live the life of a monk. They will accept that—'

'That what? That I am your mistress, and that you have brought me here to warm your bed?' When Marco talked like this, she felt as though she were listening to a stranger, Emily recognised in sharpening panic. His casual reference to 'his people' and his position as 'their future king' set him on a different plane from her, and a different life path; already he was someone else from the man she had known…a king-in-waiting…

'Are you saying that you don't want to warm it?' Marco asked her, breaking into her thoughts and then adding so seductively, almost like the old Marco that she used to know, 'Did you know there is something about the smell of your skin that right now is filling my head with the most erotic thoughts—and memories?' His voice had dropped to a whisper that was almost mesmeric. 'Can you remem-ber the first time I tasted you?'

Despite the doubts and fears she was experiencing, his words sent a thrill of sensation through her, making her body quiver with arousal at the images he was conjuring up. She wanted to tell him that she wasn't a naïve virgin any more and that she wasn't going to play his game, but instead she heard herself saying thickly,

'Yes.'

'And the first time you tasted me?'

Now she could only nod her head as desire kicked up violently inside her stomach.

Marco's fingers had encircled her wrist and he was stroking her bare skin in a rhythmic, beguiling caress.

'You didn't care then about the staff of the hotel knowing that we were lovers.'

'That was different,' she protested.

'Why?'

'Then we were private lovers. But here, Marco, as you yourself have just said, in the eyes of the people of Niroli you are their future king, and I will be your mistress.'

'So?'

Could he really not understand how she felt? Was he really already so far removed from ordinary life that he couldn't see that she would a thousand times rather be the lover of plain Marco Fierezza, than the mistress of the future King of Niroli?

'I can assure you that you will be treated with courtesy and respect, Emily, if that is what is worrying you,' he continued when she didn't answer him. 'And if it should come to my ears that you aren't, I will make sure that is corrected.'

He sounded shockingly, sickeningly, aloof and regal. The words he had spoken were the kind of statement that previously she would have laughed openly over and expected him to do the same. But she could tell from his expression that he meant them seriously. Marco's always had been a very commanding presence, but now Emily felt there was a new hauteur to his manner, a coldness and a disdain that chilled her through. The hardening of his voice and the arrogance of his stance betrayed his determination to have his own way. And a belief in his royal right to do so? Emily wasn't sure. But she did feel that the subtle change she could sense in him highlighted her own uncertainties. In London, despite the financial gap between them, they had met and lived as equals. Here, on Niroli, she knew instinctively that things would be different. But right now she was too tired to question how much that difference was going to impact on their new relationship. Right now, all she wanted… Marco was still stroking her arm. She closed her eyes and swayed closer to him. Right now, she admitted, all she wanted was this: the scented darkness, the proximity of their bodies and the promise of pleasure to come…

It was the single, sharp, shrill, animal cry of the victim of a night predator who had come down from the mountains to hunt, cut off along with its life, that woke Emily from her deep sleep. At first, her unfamiliar surroundings confused her, but then she remembered where she was. She turned over in the large bed, her body as filled with sharp dread as though the dying creature had passed on its fear to her.

'Marco?' She reached out her hand into the darkness and to the other side of the bed, but encountered only emptiness.

She had been so tired when they had arrived that she had gone straight to bed, in the room to which Marco had taken her, leaving him to explain the situation to the couple who looked after the villa for him. She suspected she must have fallen asleep within seconds of her head reaching the pillow. She had assumed though, after what he had said to her, that he would be joining her in it. She hadn't had the energy to argue, even if she had wanted to.

The door to the room's *en suite* bathroom opened. A mixture of relief and sexual tension filled her as she watched Marco walk towards her. He always slept naked and there was enough light coming in through the window to reveal the outline of his body. Her memory did the rest, filling in the shadow-cloaked detail with such powerfully loving strokes that she trembled.

'So, you're awake,' she heard him murmur as she lifted her head from the pillow to watch his approach.

'Yes.' Her response was little more than a terse, exhaled breath, an indication of her impatience at herself at being unable to tear her gaze from his magnificent physique.

'But still tired?' Marco was standing at the side of the bed now, leaning down towards her.

'A little. But not *too* tired,' she whispered daringly. She had known all along, of course, that this would be the outcome of being with him again. How could it not be when you had a man as sexually irresistible as Marco and a woman as desperately in love as she was?

They looked at one another through the semi-darkness; night sounds rustled through the room, mingling with the accelerated sound of their breathing. The darkness had become a velvet embrace, its softness pressing in on them like an intimate caress, stroking shared sensual memories over their minds.

The sudden fiercely intense surge of his own desire caught Marco off guard, as it threatened his self-control. He knew that he had missed their sex, but he hadn't been prepared for this raw, aching hunger that was now consuming him.

Emily's skin smelled of his own shower gel in a way that made him frown as his senses searched eagerly for the familiar night-warm, intimate scent that was hers and hers alone, and which he was only recognising now how much he had missed... She moved, dislodging the bedclothes, and his chest muscles contracted under the pressure of the pounding thud of his heartbeat. His pulse had started to race and he recognised that the ache of need for her, which had begun here in this bed the first night he had spent in it without her, had turned feral and taken away his control.

'Emily.'

The way he said her name turned Emily's insides to liquid

heat. He and this yearning beating up through her body were impossible to resist. She sat up in the bed, giving in to her love, pressing her lips to his bare shoulder, closing her eyes with delight as she breathed him into her. She ran the tip of her tongue along his collar-bone, feeling the responsive clench of his muscles and the reverberation of his low groan of pleasure. When he arched his neck, she kissed her way along it, caressing the swell of his Adam's apple, whilst his muscles now corded in mute recognition of his arousal. And his desire fed her own, intoxicating her, empowering her, encouraging her to make their intimacy a slow, sweetly erotic dance spiced with sudden moments of breathless intensity.

It felt good to keep their need on a tight knife-edge, refusing to let him touch her until he couldn't be refused any more, and then giving herself over completely to the touch of his hands and his mouth, crying out her need as he finally covered her and moved into her. But it was his own cry of mingled triumph and release that took them both over the edge, to the sweet place that lay beyond it.

Several minutes later, rolling away from Emily, Marco lay on his back, staring up at the ceiling and waiting for his heartbeat to steady, willing himself not to think about what his body had just told him about the intensity of his need for Emily.

If the way in which Marco was rejecting her in the aftermath of the intimacy they had just shared was hurting her, then it served her right for coming here, Emily told herself. She must take her pain and hold onto it, use it to remind herself what the reality of being here with Marco meant. It would do her good to see him in his true role, in his true habitat, because it would show her surely that the man she loved simply did not exist any more, and once she knew that her unwanted love would die. How could it not do so?

CHAPTER NINE

KING GIORGIO wagged a reproving finger. 'Is it not enough that you have deliberately attempted to undermine the authority of the Crown—an authority which is soon to be your own—with these generators you have brought to Niroli, without this added flouting of my command to end your association with this…this floozy? You know perfectly well that there are channels and protocols to be followed when a member of the royal family takes a mistress. It is unthinkable that you should have brought back with you to Niroli a woman who is a common nothing, and who never can and never will be accepted here at court!'

'You mean, I take it, that I could take my pick from the married women amongst the island's nobility? Her husband would of course be instructed to do his duty and give up his wife to royal pleasure and, in due course, both would be appropriately rewarded—the husband with an important government position, the wife with the title of Royal Mistress and a few expensive baubles.' Marco shook his head. 'I have no intention of adorning some poor courtier with a pair of horns so that I can sleep with his wife.'

'You cannot expect me to believe that you, a prince of Niroli, can be content with a woman who is a nothing—'

'Emily is far from being nothing, and the truth is that you insult her by comparing her with the blue-blooded nonentities you seem to think are so superior to her. There is no comparison. Emily is their superior in every way.' The immediate and heated ferocity of his defence of Emily and his anger against his grandfather had taken hold of Marco before he could think logically about what he was saying. His immediate impulse had been to protect her, and that alone was enough to cause him to wonder at his uncharacteristic behaviour. And yet, even though for practical and diplomatic reasons he knew if he could not bring himself to recall his statement, then at least he should temper it a little. But he couldn't do it. Why not? Was it because by bringing Emily here to Niroli he now felt a far greater sense of responsibility towards her than he had done in London?

His grandfather didn't give him time to ponder. Instead the king pushed his chair back from the table and eased himself up, before demanding regally, 'Do you really think that I am deceived by any of this, Marco? Do you think I don't realise that you have brought those generators and this woman here to Niroli expressly to anger and insult me? You may think that you can win the hearts of my people by giving them access to the technological toys you believe they crave, and that they will accept your mistress, but you are wrong. It is true that there are elements of rebellion and disaffection amongst the mountain-dwellers, the Viallis who will give you their allegiance and sell you their loyalty for the price of a handful of silver, but they are nothing. The hearts of the rest of the Nirolian population lie here with me. They, like me, know that on Niroli the old ways are the best ways, and they will show you in no uncertain terms how they feel about your attempts to win round the Viallis.'

'No, Grandfather, it is you who is wrong,' Marco answered

him curtly. 'You may wish to stick with the old ways as you call them, enforcing ignorance and poverty on people, refusing to allow them to make their own choices about the way they want to live, treating them as children. You try to rule them through fear and power, and some of them rightfully resent that, as I would do in their places. I have brought back the generators because your people, our people, need them, and I have brought Emily back because *I* need *her*.' It wasn't what he had planned to say, and it certainly wasn't what he had been thinking when he had walked into this confrontation, but as soon as he had said the words Marco recognised that they contained a truth that had previously been hidden from him. Or had it been deliberately ignored and denied by him? He had known that he wanted Emily; that he desired her and that he could make use of her presence here to underline his independence to his grandfather, but needing her…that was something else again, and it made Marco stiffen warily, ready to defend himself from what he recognised was his own vulnerability.

'The woman is a commoner, and commoners do not understand what it is to be royal. They cause problems that a woman born into the nobility would never cause.'

'You're speaking from experience?' Marco taunted his grandfather, watching as the older man's face turned a dangerously purple hue.

'You dare to suggest that I would so demean myself?'

Marco looked at him.

'Whilst Emily is here on Niroli she will be treated with respect and courtesy, she will be received at court and she will be treated in every way like the most highly born of royal mistresses,' he told his grandfather evenly. 'I have a long memory and those who do otherwise will be pursued and punished.'

He had spoken loudly enough for everyone else in the chamber to hear him, knowing that the courtiers would know as well as he did that he would soon be in a position to re-primand those who defied him now.

Before this he had never had any intention of bringing Emily to court, but he did not intend to tell his grandfather that. How dared the old man suggest that Emily was somehow less worth-while as a person than some Nirolian nobleman's wife? He'd back Emily any day if it came to having to prove herself as a person. She possessed intelligence, compassion, wit and kindness, and her natural sweetness was like manna from heaven after the falseness of the courtiers and their wives. He had seen the pleased looks that some of the flunkies had ex-changed when his grandfather had flown into a rage over the generators. Of course, they couldn't be expected to like the fact that there were going to be changes, but they were going to have to accept them, Marco decided grimly. Just as they were going to have to accept Emily. He was striding out of the audience chamber before he recognised how much more strongly he felt about protecting Emily than he had actually known…

Emily stared at her watch in disbelief. It was closer to lunchtime than breakfast! How could she have slept so late? The sensual after-ache of the night's pleasure gave her a hint of a reason for her prolonged sleep.

Marco! She sat up in bed and then saw the note he had left for her propped up on the bedside table. She picked it up and read it quickly.

He was going to the palace to see his grandfather, he had written, and since he didn't know when he would be back, he had given Maria instructions to provide her with everything she might need, and had also explained to her that Emily was going to be organising the interior renovation of the villa.

'If you feel up to it, by all means feel free to have a good look around,' he had written, 'but don't overdo things.'

There was no mention of last night, but then there was hardly likely to be, was there? What had she been hoping for? A love letter? But Marco didn't love her, did he? The starkness of that reality wasn't something she was ready to think about right now, Emily admitted. It was too soon after the traumatic recent see-sawing of her emotions from the depths of despair to the unsteady fragile happiness of Marco's appearance at the shop and their intimacy last night.

But she would have to think about it at some stage, she warned herself. After all, nothing had changed, except that she now knew what living without him felt like. She mustn't let herself forget that all this was nothing more than a small extra interlude of grace; a chance to store up some extra memories for the future.

It wouldn't do her any good to dwell on such depressing thoughts, Emily told herself. Instead, she would get up and then keep herself occupied with an inspection of the villa.

If Maria was curious about her relationship with Marco, she hid it well, Emily decided, an hour later, when she had finished a late breakfast of fresh fruit and homemade rolls, which Maria had offered her when she had come downstairs. She had eaten her light meal sitting in the warm sunlight of a second inner courtyard, and was now ready to explore the villa, which she managed to convey with halting Italian and hand-gestures to Maria, who beamed in response and nodded her head enthusiastically.

Emily had no idea when the villa had first been built, but it was obviously very old and had been constructed at a time when the needs of a household were very different from the requirements of the twenty-first century. In addition to the dark kitchen Maria showed her, there was a positive warren of passages and small rooms, providing what Emily assumed must have been the domestic service area of the house. To suit the needs of a modern family, these would have to be integrated into a much larger, lighter and more modern kitchen, with a dining area, and possibly a family room, opening out onto the courtyard.

The main doors to the villa opened into a square hallway, flanked by two good sized salons, although the décor was old-fashioned and dark.

The bedrooms either already had their own bathrooms or were large enough to accommodate *en suites*, although only the room Marco was using was equipped with relatively recent sanitary-ware.

On the top floor of the villa, there were more rooms and, by the time she had finished going round the ground and first floors, Emily was beginning to feel tired. But her tiredness wasn't stopping her from feeling excited at the prospect of taking on such a challenging but ultimately worthwhile project. The attic floor alone was large enough to convert into two self-contained units that could provide either semi-separate accommodation for older teenagers, staff quarters, or simply a bolt-hole and working area away from the hubbub of everyday family life. The courtyards to the villa were a real delight, or at least they had the potential to be. There were three of them, and the smaller one could easily be adapted to contain a swimming pool.

It was the second courtyard, which Marco's bedroom overlooked, that was her favourite, though. With giant terracotta pots filled with shrubs, palms and flowers and a loggia that ran along one wall, it was the perfect spot to sit and enjoy the peaceful sound of its central marble fountain.

Standing in it now, Emily couldn't help thinking what a wonderful holiday home the villa would make for a family. It had room to spare for three generations; with no effort at all she could see them enjoying the refurbished villa's luxurious comfort: the grandparents, retired but still very active, enjoying the company of their great-grandchildren, the kids themselves exuberant, and energetic, the sound of their laughter mingling with that of the fountain; the girls olive-skinned, pretty and dainty, the boys strongly built with their father's dark hair and shrewd gaze, the baby laughing and gurgling as Marco held him, whilst the woman who was their mother and Marco's wife—Niroli's queen—stood watching them.

Don't do this to yourself, an inner voice warned Emily. *Don't go there. Don't think about it, or her; don't imagine what it would be like to be that woman.* In reality, the home she had been busily mentally creating was not that of a king and a queen. It was the home of a couple who loved one another and their children, a home for the kind of family she admitted she had yearned for during her teenage years when she had lived with her grandfather. The kind of home that represented the life, the future, she wished desperately she would be sharing with Marco, right down to the five children. The warmth of the sun spilling into the courtyard filled it with the scent of the lavender that grew there, and Emily knew that, for the rest of her life, she would equate its scent with the pain seeping slowly through her as she acknowledged the impossibility of her dreams. If this were a fantasy, then she could magic away all those things that stood between her and Marco, and imagine a happy ending, a scenario in which he discovered that she loved him and immediately declared his own love for her. But this was real life and there was no way that was going to happen.

One day—maybe—there would be a man with whom she could find some sense of peace, a man who would give her children they could love together and cherish. But that man could not and would not be Marco, and those dark-haired girls and boys she had seen so clearly with her mind's eye, that gorgeous baby, were the children that another woman would bear for him.

And, poor things, their lives would be burdened by the weight of their royal inheritance, just as Marco's was, and that was something Emily knew she could not endure to inflict on her own babies. For them she wanted love and security and the freedom to grow into individuals, instead of being forced into the mould of royal heirs.

It was just as well that Marco had no intentions of wanting to make her his wife, on two counts, Emily told herself determinedly as she battled with her sadness, because the revealing nature of her recent thoughts had shown her what her true feelings were about Marco's royal blood. Plus, of course, as he had already told her, it was not permissible for him to marry a divorced woman.

The sound of crockery rattling on a tray and the smell of coffee brought her back to the present as Maria came into the courtyard carrying a tray of coffee for her, which she put on a table shaded from the heat of the sun by an elegant parchment-coloured sun umbrella.

Thanking her with a smile, Emily decided that she might as well start work.

Within half an hour, she was deeply engrossed in the notes she was making, having moved the coffee-pot out of the way. Although she hadn't felt nauseous this morning, the smell of the coffee had reminded her that her stomach was still queasy and not truly back to normal.

An hour later, when Marco drove into the outer courtyard, Emily was still hard at work. After leaving the palace he had been to the airport where the generators had already been unloaded. He had already made a list of those villages up in the mountains most in need of their own source of power and whilst in London he had spoken with the island's police chief and the biggest road haulier to arrange for the transport of the generators. However, whilst he had been at the airport, he had received a message from the police chief to say he had received instructions from the palace that the generators were not to be moved.

It had taken all of Marco's considerable negotiating skills, and the cool reminder that he was Niroli's future king, to persuade the police chief to change his mind and go against what he described to Marco almost fearfully as 'orders from the palace'.

Because of this Marco had decided to drive into the mountains himself to make sure that the generators were delivered safely. If his grandfather thought he could outmanoeuvre him, then he was going to have to learn the hard way that it was just not going to happen.

Marco's mouth compressed. As a successful entrepreneur whose views were respected he wasn't used to having his decisions questioned and countermanded. Had his grandfather really no idea of the potential damage he was inflicting on the island by his stubborn refusal to recognise that the world had changed and its people with it, and that it was no longer viable for a king as hugely wealthy as Niroli's to allow some of his subjects to live in conditions of severe poverty? Apart from anything else, there was the threat of civil unrest amongst the mountain-dwellers, which would be seized upon and further orchestrated by the Vialli gang that lived amongst them.

His step-grandmother had in part to be behind this, Marco decided grimly. Queen Eva was his grandfather's second wife, and it was Marco's personal opinion that she was and always had been hostile towards her predecessor's side of the family. That naturally included Marco and his two sisters. Given their step-grandmother's attitude, it was no wonder that Isabella rarely visited the palace, and that Rosa preferred not to live on the island, just as he hadn't, until recently…

* * *

Emily had been deeply engrossed in the notes she was making, but some sixth sense alerted her to Marco's presence, causing her to put down her pen and turn to look towards the entrance to the courtyard. Despite the sombreness of her earlier thoughts, the minute she saw Marco standing watching her all the feelings she had promised herself she would learn to control rushed through her. Pushing back her chair, she got up and hurried over to him.

As he watched her coming towards him Marco could feel the anger his morning had caused being eased from his body by the warmth of her welcome. He wanted to go to her and take hold of her, he wanted to take her to bed and lose himself and his problems within her. His need for her was so intense… He tensed once more. There it was again, that word need, that feeling he didn't want to have.

'What is it? What's wrong?' Emily asked him uncertainly when she saw his sudden tension.

'Nothing for you to worry about. An administrative problem I need to sort out,' he told her dismissively. 'I'll be gone for most of the afternoon.'

Emily did her best to hide her disappointment, but she knew she hadn't succeeded when she heard him exhaling irritably.

'Emily—' he began warningly.

'It's all right, I know. You're a king-in-waiting and you have far more important things to do than be with me,' she interrupted him briskly.

Marco looked at her downbent head.

'You can come with me if you wish, but it will mean a long, hot drive along dusty roads, followed by some boring delays whilst I speak with people. And since you haven't been feeling well…'

Emily wanted to tell him that being with him could never bore her, but she managed to stop herself just in time. Instead she assured him quickly, 'I'm feeling much better now. I've had a look round the villa and I could run some options by you in the car, unless…' She paused uncertainly, suddenly realising how very little she knew about what was expected of him in his new role. 'That is, will you be driving yourself, or…?'

'We aren't going on some kind of royal progress in a formal cavalcade, if that's what you mean, and, yes, I shall be driving myself,' Marco answered her. 'You'll need a hat to protect your head from the sun and a pair of sensible shoes for if you do get out of the car. Some of the villages we shall be going to are pretty remote and along single-track mountain roads. I don't want to delay too long though.' He didn't want the police chief getting cold feet and instructing the haulier to stop his fleet of lorries, or, worse, turn back.

Emily's eyes were shining as though he had offered her some kind of priceless gift, he reflected. He had a sudden impulse to take hold of her and draw her close to him, to kiss her slowly and tenderly. He shook the impulse away, not sure where it had come from or why, but knowing that it was dangerous…

CHAPTER TEN

'AM I allowed to ask any questions?' Emily said lightly. It was nearly an hour since they had left the villa. Marco had driven them through the main town and then out and up into the hills. 'Or is this trip a state secret?'

'No secret, but it is certainly a contentious issue so far as my grandfather is concerned,' Marco told her.

'If it's private family business,' she began, but Marco stopped her, shaking his head.

'No. It's very much a public business, since it involves some of the poorest communities on the island. But instead of acknowledging their need and doing something about it, my grandfather prefers to ignore it, which is why I have decided to take matters into my own hands. The more remote parts of the island do not have the benefit of electricity,' he explained. 'Because of that, these people are denied modern comforts and communication, and their children are denied access to technology and education. My grandfather believes in his divine and royal right to impose his will and keep them living as peasants. He also believes he knows what is best for them and for Niroli. Because there has been a history of insurrection amongst our mountain population, led by the Viallis, in the past, he also fears that by encouraging them to become part of today's world he will be encouraging them to challenge the Crown's supremacy.'

'And you don't agree,' Emily guessed sympathetically.

'I believe that every child has the right to a good education, and that every parent has the right to want to provide their child with the best opportunities available. My grandfather feels that by educating our poorest citizens, we will encourage them to want much more than the simple lives they presently have, he fears that some will rise up, others will desert the land and maybe even the island. But I say it's wrong to imprison them in poverty and lack of opportunity. We have a duty to them, and for me that means giving them freedom of choice. You and I know what happens when young people are disenfranchised, Emily. We have already seen it in the urban ghettos of Europe: angry young men ganging up together and becoming feral, respecting only violence and greed, because that is all they have ever known. I don't want to see that happening here.

'I have tried to persuade my grandfather to invest some of the Crown's vast financial reserves in paying to install electricity in these remote areas, but he refuses to do so. Just as he refuses to see the potential trouble he is storing up for the island.'

Emily could hear the frustration in his voice. It had touched her immensely that Marco had connected the two of them together in their shared awareness of the downsides of keeping people impoverished and powerless.

'Perhaps, once you are King…' she suggested, but Marco shook his head again.

'My grandfather is very good at imposing conditions and I don't want to trap myself in a situation where my hands are tied. Plus, it seems to me that some of Niroli's youth are already beginning to resent my grandfather's rule, just as previous generations resisted the monarchy. I do not want to inherit that resentment along with the throne, so I have decided to act now to take the heat out of the situation.'

'But what can you do?' Emily asked him uncertainly 'If your grandfather has refused to allow electricity to be supplied…'

'I can't insist that it is, no,' Marco agreed. 'But I can provide it by other means. Whilst I was in London, I bought what I hope will be enough generators to at least provide some electricity for the villages. My grandfather is furious, of course, but I am hoping that he will back down and accept what I have done as a way of allowing him to change his mind without losing face. He is an old man who has ruled autocratically all his life. It is hard for him, I know that, but the Crown has to change or risk having change forced upon it.'

'You think there will be some kind of uprising?' Emily was horrified, instantly thinking of the danger that would bring to Marco.

'Not immediately. But the seeds are there. And still my grandfather is so determined to hold absolute power.'

'You pretend not to do so, but in reality you understand him very well, and I think you feel a great deal of compassion for him, Marco,' Emily said gently.

'On the contrary, what I feel is a great deal of irritation and anger because he refuses to see the danger he is courting,' Marco corrected her. Her perceptiveness had startled him, making him feel that she knew him rather better than he had realised. 'There are so many changes I want to make, Emily, so much here for me to do, but my grandfather blocks me at every turn.'

'You've lived away from the island for a long time and you've grown used to making your own decisions without the need to consult others. Perhaps your grandfather is being difficult because he sees this and in some ways he fears it—and you. You said yourself that he's an old man—he obviously knows that he can't continue to be King, but my guess is that he doesn't want to acknowledge that publicly, and that a part of him wants to continue to rule Niroli through you. When you come up with your own plans and they are opposed to his, he tries to block you because he's afraid of losing his power to you.'

'I doubt you would ever get him to admit any of that.'

Emily could hear the frustration in Marco's voice and, with it, his hunger to right what he saw as wrongs. He would be a strong king morally, socially, politically and in all the other important ways, she recognised. Listening to him had brought home to her the reality of her own situation. Even if by some miracle he should return her love, there was no future for them. She could not be his queen, and she could never do anything that would prevent him from being Niroli's king. Not now, after hearing him speak so passionately about his country and his people. If Marco had a duty to his people, then she too had duties to him and her love for him; loving someone meant putting them first and their needs before one's own. Marco's great need was to fulfil his duty and he could not do that with her in his life. A small, sad shadow darkened her eyes—the ghost of her dreams. Seeing it, Marco frowned.

'I'm boring you,' he announced curtly.

'No,' Emily told him. 'No! I like listening to you talking about your plans. I just wish that you had told me who you were when we first met.' Had he done so, she would have been so much better armoured against her vulnerability to him, and she would certainly never have started dreaming they could have a permanent future together.

'It wasn't a deliberate deceit on my part,' Marco defended himself coolly.

'Maybe not, but you could have said something… warned me. Then, at least…' She stopped, shaking her head, not wanting to admit her own folly where he was concerned.

'In order to live the kind of life I wanted, to prove myself on my own terms, it was necessary for me to do it with anonymity and without the trappings of royalty.

'I grew up here as a renegade in my grandfather's eyes. I was his heir, but I refused to conform or let him turn on me and bully me the way he did my father.' Marco's expression changed, and Emily ached to reach out and comfort him when she saw that look in his eyes.

'My father was too gentle to stand up to my grandfather. As a child, I hated knowing that. As a form of compensation, I suppose, I rebelled against my grandfather's authority and I swore that I would prove to him, and to the world, that I had the capability to succeed as myself.'

'But while you were proving yourself, you missed the island and your family, your father?' Emily guessed tenderly.

Marco opened his mouth to reject her words and then admitted huskily,

'Yes. It was such a shock when he was killed in a freak accident off the island's coast. Something I'd never imagined happening…never considered.'

And along with his natural grief at the loss of his father, Marco had had to deal with the irreversible changes in his own circumstances that had followed, Emily acknowledged silently. It must have been so hard for him—a man used to taking control of every aspect of his personal life, to have to come to terms with the fact that, as King, a huge part of his life would now be beyond his control. Just listening to him was causing a change within her own thoughts, turning her angry bitterness and pain into compassionate understanding and acceptance. It altered everything for her. Did he recognise how very alone he was emotionally? Was that a deliberate choice, or an accidental one? If he knew about it, did he care, or did he simply accept it as part of the price he paid for his royal status?

'I would hate to be in your shoes.' The words had slipped out before she could stop them.

Marco looked searchingly at her.

'What do you mean?' he demanded.

'I can hear how important your people are to you, Marco, and how strongly you feel about helping them, but...' She paused and shook her head. 'I couldn't pay the price you're about to pay for being Niroli's king. On the one hand, yes, you will have enormous wealth and power, but on the other you won't have any personal freedom, any right to do what you want to do. Every-thing will have to be weighed against how it affects your people. That is such a tremendously heavy responsibility.' She gave a small sigh. 'I suppose it's different if you're born to it. I'm beginning to see why princes marry princesses,' she added ruefully. 'You really do have to be born royal to understand.'

'Not necessarily. You're doing a pretty good job of showing you have a strong grasp of what's involved,' Marco told her dryly. They had rarely spoken so openly to one another and it surprised him how much he valued what she had said to him. Impulsively, he slowed the car and reached for her hand, giving it a small squeeze that caused her to look at him in surprise. Such a small, tender gesture was so very unlike him.

'I'm glad you're here with me, Emily.'

Her heart was thumping and thudding with the sweetness of the emotions pouring through her. Marco brought the car briefly to a halt and leaned across and kissed her—a hard, swift kiss that contained a message she couldn't manage to decipher, but which sent a physical craving for him soaring through her body. She had never, ever known him exhibit such extraordinarily un-Marco behaviour before. Her heart felt as though it had wings, her own happiness dizzying her.

She mustn't let a casual moment out of time lead her into

forgetting what she had just recognised, she warned herself. But, then, should she let what she knew to be their separate futures prevent her from enjoying their shared here and now? a different voice coaxed.

'At this stage of the game, when you've got so much to deal with, it's only natural that you need someone to bounce ideas off and confide in,' she told him, 'and…' She paused, unsure of just how much she dared say without giving herself away completely.

'And?' Marco probed as they bounced along the narrow track past a cluster of small houses.

'And I wouldn't want that someone to be anyone else but me,' Emily told him simply.

A young man, tall and gangly and outgrowing his clothes, was standing in the middle of the road in front of Marco's car waving his hands, his face alight with excitement.

Emily looked questioningly at Marco.

'Tomasso,' he informed her as he brought the car to a halt. 'He is the leader of a gang of young Vialli hotheads, and he is also the person I have chosen to be my representative in taking care of the generator and introducing his village to its benefits.'

The moment Marco opened the car door and got out, Tomasso bounded up to him exclaiming, 'Highness, Highness, it is here! The generator, just as you promised. We have built a special place for it. Let me show you…'

An elderly woman appeared from the nearest house, tutting and looking very disapproving as she came over to join them.

'What is this—where is your respect for our Crown?' she demanded. 'Highness, forgive my thought-less grandson,' Emily could hear her saying as she curtseyed to Marco.

This was a side of him she had never seen, Emily thought to herself as Marco leaned forward and assisted the elderly woman to her feet, accepting her homage with easy grace, whilst maintaining a very specific formal dignity that Emily could see the elderly woman liked. As more villagers surrounded him, he was very much the future king, so much so that Emily's emotions blocked her throat. She felt so proud sitting in the car watching him and yet, at the same time, so painfully distanced from him. What she was witnessing was making her even more aware of how impossible it would be for them to sustain a long-term relationship. Already she could see the curious and even hostile glances being directed towards her, and she guessed when Marco turned to look at the car that he was being asked who she was.

She looked away, her gaze caught by an array of brightly painted and beaded leather purses spilling out of a basket, just outside the door to one of the houses. Her artist's eye could immediately see how, with some discreet direction, highly desirable objects could be made by adapting the leather and bead-work to cover boxes. She was constantly on the lookout for such accessories to dress her decorating schemes; they walked out of her shop faster than she could buy them. She made a mental note to ask Marco a bit more about the leather-work and those who produced it.

It was nearly half an hour before he returned to the car, having been pressed into going and viewing the generator in its new home. When he returned he was accompanied by a group of laughing young men, whilst Emily noticed the older people of the village held back a little, still eyeing her warily. One of them, a bearded and obviously very old man, went up to Marco and said something to him, shaking his head and pointing to the car. Emily saw the way Marco's expression hardened as he listened.

'What was that old man saying to you?' she asked him, once he was back in the car and they had driven out of the village.

'Nothing much.'

'Yes, he was. He was saying something about me, wasn't he?' Emily pressed him. 'He didn't like you tak-ing me there.'

Marco looked at her. Rafael, the elder of the village, was very much his grandfather's man. He did not approve of the generator and had said so, and then, when he had seen Emily in the car, he had berated Marco for—as he had put it— 'bringing such a woman to Niroli'. 'Where is her shame?' Rafael had demanded. 'She shows her face here as boldly as though she has none. In my day, such a woman would have known her place. It is an insult to us, the people of Niroli, that you have brought her here,' he had told Marco fiercely.

'Rafael has a reputation as someone with very strong views. He is even older than my grandfather and tends to think of himself as the guardian of the island's morals…'

'You mean he disapproves of me being here with you,' Emily guessed.

Marco was negotiating a tight bend, and Emily had to wait for him to answer her.

'What he thinks or feels is his business. What I choose to do is my own,' he told her grimly.

But the reality was that it wasn't, and that whatever Marco chose to do *was* the business of the people of Niroli.

In an attempt to change the subject, she asked him brightly,

'I saw a basket of leather purses…'

'Yes, the women of the villages make them. They sell them to tourists, if they can, although these days the visitors who come to Niroli would far rather have a designer piece than something fashioned out of home-made leather.'

'Mmm…I was thinking that, with a bit of time and effort, the leather could be used to cover trinket boxes, the bead or-namentation was so pretty, and I know from my own experi-ence there is a huge market for that kind of thing. If, as you say, the villagers are short of money, then…'

'It's worth thinking about, but there's no way I want my people involved in any kind of exploitation.'

'It was only a thought.'

'And a good one. Leave it with me.'

When the time came for him to marry, Marco reflected, he would need a wife who would take on the role of helping him to help his people. Emily could easily fulfil that role. Somehow, that thought had slipped under his guard and into his head where it had no right to be. Just as he had no right to allow Emily into his heart. *Into his heart?* Now, *what* was he thinking? Just because Rafael's objection to her presence had made him feel so angry and protective of her, that didn't mean that she had found her way into his heart. Did it?

CHAPTER ELEVEN

EMILY sighed to herself as she parked the car Marco had hired for her to use whilst she was staying on Niroli outside the island's elegant spa. Although he had made love to her last night and it was at his suggestion that she was visiting the spa today, she knew that she would far rather have had his company. Marco, though, was too busy with royal affairs to spend time with her. His purchase and distribution of the generators had led to yet another row with his grandfather, which had resulted in Emily asking Marco if there wasn't someone within his family who could mediate between the two of them.

'Someone, you mean, like my sister Isabella?' he had replied. 'She claims that my grandfather doesn't value her because she is female. No, Emily.' He had shaken his head. 'This is something I have to deal with myself.'

To Emily's relief, she had now gone three whole days without being sick, although she had noticed that, despite the fact that she wasn't eating very much, the waistline of one of her favourite skirts was now uncomfortably tight, and even more uncomfortable were her breasts, which felt swollen and tender. It must be due to too-rapid a change of climate, she had told herself this morning as she'd dressed.

Marco had told her that the spa was owned and run by

Natalia Carini, daughter of Giovanni, the Royal Vine-keeper. Emily had been a bit hesitant about coming here and putting herself forward for 'inspection' when she was at her most vulnerable. But as she walked into the spa foyer she heard the pretty girl behind the reception desk saying to another client, 'I'm sorry, but Miss Carini isn't here today.'

Emily hadn't really been sure how she felt about meeting someone who might have known Marco when he was younger. Like any woman in love, she longed to know everything there was to know about him and yet, at the same time, the reality of her position in his life made her feel that she wanted to remain anonymous. In London, it might be acceptable for a couple to live together as lovers without any intention of making their relationship permanent, but she suspected that things were different here on Niroli—even if Marco weren't who he was and destined to be King and, no doubt, to make a dynastic marriage.

'May I help you?'

Emily returned the receptionist's smile. 'I don't have an appointment, but I was wondering if it was possible to have a treatment?'

'Since it isn't the height of the tourist season yet, we should be able to fit you in. What kind of treatment would you like? We specialise here in using natural substances, especially the island's own volcanic mud. It's very therapeutic, especially when we use it in conjunction with our specially designed massage treatments.

'Here's a list of the treatments we offer, and a medical questionnaire.' The girl smiled again. 'The owner of the spa takes her responsibility to our clients very seriously, and I should point out to you that some of the more vigorous massages are not suitable for women who are pregnant.'

Pregnant! Emily almost laughed. Well, she certainly

wasn't. And then suddenly it hit her, her brain mentally registering the facts and assembling them: her sickness, her aching breasts, her growing waist… A wave of sickening shock and disbelief thundered through her, and she could hear the receptionist asking her anxiously if she was all right.

'I'm…fine…' she lied.

But of course she wasn't. She was anything but. How could she be 'fine', when the reason for the sickness she'd been suffering these last few weeks, and the fact that, oddly, her waist seemed to have expanded making her clothes feel tight, had suddenly been made blindingly obvious to her?

Was she right? Was she pregnant? She did some hasty mental calculations, whilst her heart banged anxiously against her ribs.

She needed very badly to sit down, but not here. Not anywhere where the truth might out and there could be any hint of a threat to her unborn child. It had only been seconds, minutes at the most, since she had realised the reality, but already she knew that there was nothing she would not do to protect the new life growing inside her. She would allow nothing or no one to imperil her child's safety and right to life!

Emily stared at her own reflection in the bedroom mirror and tried not to panic. There was little to show that she was pregnant as yet, apart from that slight thickening of her waist, but how much longer would she have before Marco became suspicious? She couldn't afford to be still here on Niroli by then. Her throat went dry. Inside her head she could hear Marco's voice telling her, at the very beginning of their relationship, that there would be no accidents, and what he expected her to do if one occurred.

Of course, what he had meant and not said was that he didn't want any royal bastards.

But there was no way she could destroy her child. She would rather destroy herself.

However, logically, Emily knew that, even if Marco had not made it plain he did not want her to have his child, there would be no place here on Niroli for the future king's pregnant mistress, or his illegitimate baby! What on earth was she going to do? She had never felt more alone.

'And now the village elder says that his orders have been ignored, and that the generator-shed has been broken into and the generator itself stolen. You see what you have done, what trouble you have caused by your interference?'

Marco forced himself to count slowly to ten before responding to his grandfather's angry but also triumphant accusations.

'You say that Rafael gave orders that the shed housing the generator was to be boarded up for the safety of the villagers. What is that supposed to mean?'

One of his grandfather's aides bent his head close to the Royal Ear and murmured something in it.

'The peace of the village was being destroyed—by the noise of the generator and various electrical appliances. Several villagers had complained to him that it had put their hens off laying and stopped their cows producing milk.'

Marco didn't know whether to laugh or cry. 'And because of *that* he stopped the villagers using the generator?' he demanded incredulously. 'No wonder they decided to ignore him!'

'Rafael says that he has long had concerns about the rebellious Vialli tendencies amongst this group of young men. Now that they have stolen the generator and are refusing to say where it is, he has had no other option but to order that they are punished.'

'*What?*'

'Furthermore, Rafael has told me his village is on the verge of anarchy, and that it will spread to other villages in the mountains.'

'This is crazy,' Marco told his grandfather. 'If anyone should be locked up, it's Rafael with his prehistoric views. Grandfather, you must see how foolish it was for him to have done this,' Marco implored. His grandfather was after all an educated, astute and wily man, whilst Rafael was a simple peasant.

'What I see is that you are the cause of this trouble with your reckless refusal to obey my commands.'

Marco didn't trust himself to stay and listen to any more, in case it provoked him into open warfare with his grandfather and his outdated ideas. Giving King Giorgio a small, formal half-bow, he then turned on his heel and strode out of the room.

In the corridors dust motes danced on the warm afternoon air. Emily would be back at the villa by now. An image of her slid into his head: she would be sitting in the shade, and when she saw him walking towards her she would look up at him and give him that welcoming smile. She would also look cool and calm, and just seeing her would take the edge off his own frustration. Right now, he admitted, he would give anything to share his experiences of the morning with her. Emily, with her understanding and her sympathetic ear—he needed both of those very badly.

He paused. There it was again, that word, 'need'. It suddenly struck him how very alone he would be feeling right now if Emily hadn't been here on Niroli with him. It was only since bringing her to the island that he had recognised how good she was with people, and at problem-solving, and how much it meant to him to have the safety valve of being able to talk openly to her about the situation with his grandfather. Increasingly he was beginning to feel that he didn't want her to leave either the island or his bed. But whilst he might flout the royal rules for the benefit of his people, where his personal life was concerned he couldn't do the same and succeed. The only way he could keep Emily on the island was by elevating her to the position of Royal Mistress, and to do that he would have to procure a suitably noble husband for her, one who understood the way in which these things were done. Whilst he knew he would be able to find such a husband, he also knew that Emily would refuse point-blank to enter that kind of marriage and, besides... Besides what? He didn't *want* her to have a husband...

He had no time to delve into the inner workings of his mind at the moment, he reminded himself; nor could he go back to the villa—and Emily—no matter how much he wanted to do so. First he must go up to Rafael's village and deal with the situation there before it got any worse. And what about his growing dependence on Emily? When was he going to deal with that—before it got worse?

'Emily.'

She tensed as she heard Marco call out her name as he came out into the sheltered inner courtyard, where she was seated in the shade, one hand lying protectively against her stomach as she tried to come to terms with everything.

It was early evening and she could hear the sharp edge of something unfamiliar in his voice. What was it? Not tiredness or irritation, and certainly not anxiety, but somehow a *something* that made her heart ache for him, above and beyond her own pain and fear for herself and their child. Was it always going to be like this? Was she always going to have this instinctive need to give him the best of her love? How could she do so now?

'I would have been back earlier,' Marco told her, 'but I had to go up to Rafael's village to put an end to some trouble brewing there, as my grandfather informed me with great delight earlier.'

'What kind of trouble?' Emily asked anxiously.

Marco sat down next to her. She could smell the dusty heat

of the day on him, but under it she was, as always, acutely conscious of the scent that was so sensually him. However, this evening, instead of filling her with desire, it filled her with a complex mix of emotions so intense that they clogged her throat with tears—tears for their baby, who would never know and recognise his father's scent, tears for herself because she would have to live without Marco. But, most of all, tears for Marco himself, because he could never share with her the unique feeling that came from knowing they had created a life together. Her child, their child, his first-born child. The huge tremor of emotion that seized her shook her whole body, overwhelming her with a flood of love and pain in equal proportions. She wanted this baby—his child—so very much. Its conception might have been wholly unplanned, but if she could go back and change things she knew that she would not do so. She was a modern woman, financially independent, with her own home and her own business, and more than enough love to give to her baby. A baby that would never know its father's love, she reminded herself as Marco answered her question, forcing her to focus on what he was saying and to put her own thoughts to one side.

'Rafael had tried to stop the villagers using the generator,' he explained. 'So Tomasso and some of his friends rebelled and hijacked it. Then Rafael—with my grandfather's approval—had the young fools punished. They were already antagonistic towards a way of life that traps them in the past and my grandfather's old-fashioned determination to enforce a way of life on them to their detriment.'

'It can't be good that they feel so disenfranchised,' Emily felt bound to comment.

'I know,' Marco acknowledged. 'If my grandfather was more reasonable, I could discuss with him my concern that these youngsters could, if handled the wrong way, become so disaffected that ultimately it could result in civil unrest and even violence. But the minute I tell him that, his reaction will be to have them imprisoned.'

'You need to find a way of getting them onside and opening a dialogue with them that allows them to feel their concerns are being addressed,' Emily offered.

'My views exactly,' Marco agreed. 'I've told them that it's an issue I intend to take on board once I take over from my grandfather and I've asked them to be patient until then. But I also know that the moment I start instituting any reforms, the old guard is going to react against them, because my grandfather has drip-fed them the fear that change means that they will lose out in some way.'

Emily listened sympathetically. She could see how passionately Marco felt about the situation. But she also sensed that the more angry and opposed to his grandfather Marco became, the less chance there was of them reaching a mutually acceptable solution.

'I don't have to tell you that your grandfather is an old man,' she replied. 'It may be that his pride won't allow him to admit that he has got things wrong and they've gone too far, or that the way the island is ruled needs to change. You might have to back-track a little, Marco, and find a way to offer him a face-saving way of accepting your changes. Maybe you could handle them in such a way that he could feel they were his ideas—in public at least.' She could see from Marco's expression that he wasn't willing to take on board what she was saying. It seemed to her that he and his grandfather were two very proud and stubborn men and that neither was prepared to give in to the other.

'You haven't seen anything of the island yet,' he told her abruptly. 'We'll remedy that tomorrow.' For Emily's benefit, or for his own, because he needed to put some distance between himself and his grandfather?

CHAPTER TWELVE

'ARE you sure you've got time to do this?' Emily queried as Marco held open the door of the car for her before they set off to see something of the island. The morning sunshine cast sharp patterns on the worn flagstones of the courtyard and Emily was glad of the welcome coolness of the air-conditioned car. Hadn't she read somewhere that pregnancy increased the blood flow and made one feel warmer? Pregnancy. She ached to be able to share her joy with Marco and yet, at the same time, she was also afraid of his reaction. If he should try to pressure her into having a termination it would break her heart, but, logically, what else could he do? Even if he was prepared to understand and accept that she wanted to have this baby and bring it up alone, she suspected that his grandfather would be totally opposed to the idea. The old king would surely put pressure on Marco to deal with her. She didn't want to put Marco in that position and she wanted to keep her child as far away as possible from what increasingly she felt was a very negative kind of environment. The Nirolian royal family might be the richest in the world, but so far as Emily was concerned they seemed to be as dysfunctional as they were wealthy. Money wasn't important to her, so long as she had enough for her needs. She wanted her child to grow up confident that he or she was rich in love rather than money. What she wanted, she admitted, was for her child to be raised somewhere very far away from Niroli and without the burden of being a royal bastard. So what was she going to do? Return to London without telling Marco she was having his child?

That was certainly her easiest option, Emily felt. But did she have the strength to do it? Could she walk away from Marco without telling him? She loved her child enough already to do whatever she had to do to protect him or her, including leaving the man she adored; she knew that, almost without having to think about it. However, did she also love Marco enough to spare him the necessity of having to take on board prospective fatherhood and the problems that would cause for him? Was she strong enough to deny her instinctive longing to share her news with him, even though she knew he couldn't, and wouldn't, share her growing joy at the prospect of having his baby?

It was an extraordinarily wonderful gift that fate was giving her: a child, and not just any child, but the seed of the man she loved. She could picture him now; somehow Emily already knew that her baby would be a boy. He would have Marco's features and perhaps a little of his arrogance. He would look at her with Marco's eyes and she would melt with love for him and the man who had fathered him. And, later, when he was old enough to demand his father's name? She would deal with that when it happened. For now, what concerned her most was her baby's health and whether she could leave Niroli without Marco suspecting anything. So how was she going to do that? She couldn't just tell him she didn't want him any more. He would never believe her.

Perhaps he would believe her if she told him she wasn't comfortable with her role in his life. She wasn't even his formally recognised mistress, and she felt it could reflect on her business reputation. Marco's own pride meant that he would be able to identify with that. Last night, when they had made love, he hadn't questioned the way she had encouraged him to gentle his possession of her, holding her breath a little, caught as she was between her maternal anxiety for her baby and the intense physical desire he always aroused in her. But Marco was a skilled and a sensual lover, who knew every single one of her body's responses and how to invoke them. There was no way he wouldn't soon notice a new desire on her part to make his penetration of her less intense.

A small, sad semi-smile touched her lips. Marco didn't know it yet, but the sightseeing journey they were taking together today could well be the last they would make together. Now she was destined to set out on a new path, which she would share with this gift he had given her.

'Seat belt,' Marco reminded her. He reached across to secure the belt for her, before she could stop him. Immediately Emily breathed in, protectively. There was no bump of any kind to betray her, but still she felt a sharp clutch of anxiety for the vulnerability of her child. It would be like this for the rest of her life, she recognised. No matter that one day this baby she had conceived so unintentionally would be an adult; as a mother she would always be fiercely protective. Though, of course, there would be many things she could not protect her child from, foremost amongst which would be the pain of knowing his father hadn't wanted him.

'Emily?'

To her shock, Marco had placed his hand flat against her belly. Fearfully she turned to look at him. Had he, by some intuitive means, actually guessed?

'You're looking so much better than you did when you first arrived here,' she heard him tell her. 'Niroli's sunshine has done you good.'

Shakily, Emily released her pent-up breath. He hadn't guessed; it was just her own anxiety that was making her think that he must have done.

'I don't think anyone wouldn't enjoy it. I know I haven't seen much of the island…'

'Today, we're going to see as much of it as we can,' Marco told her as he started the car, 'and my royal duties will just have to wait.'

Whatever else the future held for Marco's child, she was glad that it wouldn't be the dark shadow of duty that fell across Marco's life, Emily decided emotionally. The little boy might have to grow up not knowing his father, but he would be free of the burden Marco carried, and she was passionately grateful for that. Though, at the same time, almost overwhelmed by the intensity of her love for Marco, she reflected as he turned the car off the main road into a much narrower lane that ran close to the high, rocky coastline where cliffs plunged down into the sea.

'This was one of my favourite places when I was a boy,' Marco confided as he stopped the car.

Emily could understand why. There was an elemental wildness about it; in some ways, the landscape matched the man.

'Come on, let's get out of the car.'

Emily wasn't sure she wanted to. The height of the cliffs gave her an uncomfortable feeling of vertigo. But she could see that Marco was determined and she didn't want to have to explain to him how she felt.

'I used to come here and gaze out to sea, and promise myself that one day I'd get away from here and from my grandfather. But, of course, even then I knew that ultimately I would have to come back,' Marco confessed, once they were standing a few feet back from the edge of the cliff-top. He bent down and picked up a handful of the thin, stony soil that lay at the roots of the weather-beaten gorse bushes that grew in such abundance along this part of the coast, and flung it as far out to sea as he could.

Watching him, Emily knew that this was a re-enactment of something he had done many times as a boy—as a way of releasing the anger inside him? It was an emotion he had partially dissipated by leaving the island and making a life for himself. But it would never really leave him so long as he and his grandfather struggled for supremacy one over the other. And whilst they were embroiled in that struggle, others would suffer. She could not allow her child to be one of them...

All of a sudden it hit her: she *had* to tell Marco that she intended to leave. She couldn't stop herself from reaching out to touch him and placed her hand on his bare forearm. Immediately he turned towards her.

'Marco,' she began tentatively, and then stopped. Unexpectedly he reached for her and took her in his arms, kissing her with such fiercely sweet passion that it made her eyes sting with tears.

Why was he doing this? Marco asked himself. He knew that it couldn't go on. Already, deep down inside, he knew he was becoming too dependent on her, and she was becoming too important to him. That couldn't be allowed to happen. There was no room in his life for that kind of relationship with her. He was Niroli's future king and he intended to devote every ounce of his mental and physical energy to his country and its people. He would break down the restrictions that centuries of royal rule had placed, he would open the door for Niroli's population to walk freely into the new century. There was no legitimate place in his life for the kind of relationship he had with Emily. He was reeling at the way he felt about her now, the intensity that was being demanded of him. It was only recently he had started to feel like this, to recognise there was within him this dangerous need to have her close, a need that went far beyond any kind of sexual desire. But such emotion could not be allowed to exist, it could not be given a name, or a place in his life.

He started to pull away from her and then stopped, smothering a savage groan before he tightened his hold on her and kissed her again.

Emily's mouth felt soft and giving beneath his own, her body warm, and he longed to possess her and fill her and lose himself in her and know the passion of loving her.

'Marco!' Emily objected, somehow managing to stem her own longing and drag her mouth from beneath his. She was trembling from head to foot, afraid not of him but of herself and the intensity of her feelings, and stumbling over the words in her desperation.

'There's no easy way to say this, but the truth is that I should never have come here. Niroli is different from London, and my role in your life has changed. I can't live like this, Marco, a semi-secret mistress, despised and ignored by the court, and forced to live in the shadows. I'm going back to the UK just as soon as it can be arranged. It will be best for both of us.'

She was only saying what he already knew to be true, and yet he felt as shocked as though his guts had been splintered with ice picks. She couldn't do this! He wasn't ready to let her go. He needed her here with him. He should, he knew, be feeling relieved, but instead he felt more as though he had suffered a mortal blow. Pain rolled over him in mind-numbing waves, crashing through him and drowning out reason, spreading its unbearable agony to every part of him. He could hardly think for it, do anything other than try somehow to survive its rapacious teeth as it savaged him and tormented him. How could this have happened? How could he be experi-

encing this? The thoughts and feelings that filled him were
so new and unfamiliar that they made him feel as though he
was suddenly a stranger to him-self. He felt like a man possessed by…by what? He shook his head, unable to allow the
word pulsing in his heart to form. He had wanted it to happen,
he had wanted her to leave. But not like this… He'd wanted
to be the one to tell her to go… But how? That he didn't want
her here because he was afraid that she would come between
him and his duty? His whole body shuddered as the pain
savaged it once more.

Why didn't Marco say something, anything? Emily
worried anxiously.

What could she say without risking betraying the truth?

'I loved the life we shared together in London, Marco. But
things are different here. The time we're sharing together is
borrowed time, stolen time, perhaps,' she told him sadly. 'It's
better that I go now.'

Marco could feel the heavy drum of his heartbeat thudding
out a requiem for their relationship as he heard the finality in
her voice.

'There'll never be anyone else in my life like you, Marco,
nor a relationship to match the one we've shared.'

The words felt as though they were being ripped from her
like a layer of her skin, but she couldn't hold them back; they
were after all the truth, even though she knew she was a fool
for having said them.

But it didn't matter now that she was compounding that
error by lifting her hand to his face, tears burning at the backs
of her eyes as she felt the familiar texture that was hard with
the beginnings of his beard against the softness of her palm.

'Emily.'

He had caught hold of her hand before she could stop him,
lifting it to his lips and then dropping it when he felt her

tremble, to pull her bodily into his arms and then plunder her mouth with his own. Not that she made any attempt to resist him. Instead, she gave him the sweetness he was demanding whilst she clung helplessly to him.

Few people visited this part of the island, and Marco realised that an irresistible need was flooding through him to know the intimacy of sex on this wild headland. He couldn't let her go without this one last time, a final memory he would have to make last a lifetime of days and nights once he was without her. There had been many many times when their pleasure had been more sensual and more sustained, when he had deliberately set himself the task of pleasing her. But no time had ever been more intense than this, or more emotional. Because this was the last time that finally he could give to himself what he had previously so rigidly denied, and that was the right to feel with his emotions what he was feeling with his flesh.

This was too much, Emily told herself. She just wasn't strong enough to endure this kind of passion. It was as though Marco had wrenched away, with his clothes, the barrier she had always sensed he kept raised against her.

As they lay together on the lavender-scented turf, the sun warming their naked bodies, the kisses he lavished on her body were hot and fierce with a desire that went beyond the merely physical. As though by shared consent, neither of them spoke. What words were there to say, after all? Emily wondered, with dry-eyed hurt. Words would only be lies, or, worse, create wounds. It was better this way, that their last memory of one another was one filled with a shared but unspoken awareness of what they'd shared and what they would never have again. It seemed to Emily as she touched him that she had never loved him more. Something within her, that was maybe both lover and prospective mother, swelled her heart with bitter-sweet emotion.

They kissed and touched, their lips clinging, their bodies urgent, trying desperately to hold onto every second of their pleasure. But, like sand, it could not be held, running swiftly through their fingers instead as Emily's cries of pleasure became soft sighs of contentment.

She would treasure her memories of this day for the rest of her life.

She smiled lazily up at Marco as he leaned over her.

'I don't want you to leave.'

Marco had no idea where the words had come from. No! That was lie. He knew exactly where they had come from and why. And even if he hadn't, the heavy pounding of his heart would have told him. What on earth was he doing, when he had already decided that she must go? What had happened to him to make him want to change his mind on the strength of a few minutes of good sex? he derided himself. But it wasn't the good sex he didn't want to lose—it was Emily herself.

Emily wondered if anything else in her life could ever be as poignant as this. Marco had never, ever asked her for anything, never mind pleaded with her so emotionally! She so wanted to fling herself into his arms and cover his face with passionately joyful kisses as she told him there was nothing she wanted more than to be with him. But how could she?

'Marco, I'm sorry. I can't.' Her voice was little more than an anguished whisper, but Marco heard it, releasing her abruptly and turning away from her. She knew how much it must have cost him to ask her to stay. Given his inbuilt sense of male arrogance and his pride, along with his background and upbringing, she could only marvel that he had.

She got to her feet and said his name unsteadily, but he was already heading back to the car.

'Marco!' she protested. 'Please listen to me…'

He stopped walking and turned around. She saw his chest

lift as he breathed in sharply and the sadness that filled her was not just for herself, but for both of them. She knew what she had to do, where her responsibility now lay, but how could she walk away letting him think that she hadn't wanted to stay with him? She couldn't, she decided frantically. Yes, she had her baby to think of and, yes, she was afraid of Marco's reaction to the news that she was pregnant. But she loved Marco, too, and the knowledge that he wanted her enough to actually ask her to stay was too sweetly precious that she couldn't deny its tremendous effect on her.

She still had to leave, nothing could change that, but she knew she couldn't go away from him without telling him why it was so important that she went.

She took a deep breath; this was the most difficult thing she had ever had to do. 'I don't *want* to leave you, Marco. But I *have* to. You see, I'm having your child. I'm pregnant.'

What? Marco could feel her words exploding inside his skull as he battled with his own disbelief.

'I know you told me at the beginning of our relationship that there must not be any accidents,' Emily continued, carefully cutting into the tension of his complete silence, 'and...and of course I understand now why you said that. The future King of Niroli's bastard isn't the title I want for our baby.' She gave a small shrug. 'The truth is, I don't want him to have any title at all, and if there is one thing in all of this that I am grateful for, it's that our son won't ever have to live the kind of controlled and confined life you will have to live. What I want for him more than anything else is the kind of personal freedom that you don't have and that you can't give to your legitimate children. I want him to grow up in a home filled with love, where what matters most is that he finds his own sense of where his life lies and how his talents should be used. I don't want his future to be corrupted by wealth and position. I don't want him to have to carry the burdens I can see you carrying, Marco. I can't give him his father, but I can give him the right to define his own life, and to me that heritage is of far more value than anything your legitimate children will inherit.'

For a few seconds, Marco was too taken aback by what she had said to speak. From the moment of his birth he had been brought up to be aware of the tremendous importance of his role and his family. The thought that someone was not awed and impressed by it was something he found hard to take in. But he could see that Emily meant what she'd said. Senses of isolation and aloneness, of having lost something he could never regain, an awareness that somehow, somewhere, he had turned his back on something precious stabbed through him. With it came the drift of painful memories: of himself as a young boy longing passionately for the freedom to be himself. He could see his father's struggles and his mother's anguish and, of course, his grandfather's anger. He could also hear the echo of his own childishly piping voice stating defiantly, 'When I am grown up and I can do what I want, I won't be a prince!' But with a kick like an iron-tipped boot, slowly but surely his position and its claims on him had reshaped him. He pictured two small boys, both dark-haired and sturdy, one of them grubby and laughing as he played happily with his friends. The other was sad-eyed and alone, held at a respectful distance by his peers, protected by privilege, or was he imprisoned by it?

What folly was this? Marco forced back the memories, refusing to acknowledge them any more, letting his pride take over instead. 'You are being naïve. No one else will share your views, Emily. In fact, they will think you a fool. And, besides, being King of Niroli is about more than any of those things,' he retaliated sharply. 'It's about making a difference to my people, it's about leading them to a better future. Do you really think our son, my son, will thank you for denying him his birthright?'

'He has no birthright here on Niroli. I am your mistress, and he will be illegitimate.'

'He has the birthright I choose to give him.'

'By recognising him and making him face the world as less than your children born within royal wedlock? By making him grow up in an environment where he will always be beneath them—in their eyes and, ultimately, in his own?'

'He will be a member of the Niroli royal family, how can you think of denying him that? Do you really think he will thank you when he is old enough to know what he has lost?'

In the space of a few heated sentences, they had become opponents, Emily recognised.

'It doesn't matter how much we argue about our own feelings,' she told him. 'You are not yet King Marco, and I doubt that your grandfather would welcome the birth of an illegitimate child to a woman of such lowly status as me.'

There was just enough edge to her voice to warn Marco that, at some stage, she had learned of his grandfather's opinion of her.

'The fact that I am his father automatically gives him his own status,' Marco retaliated, and then realised his words had added to Emily's fury rather than soft-ened it.

'Yes, as your bastard—a royal bastard, I know. But he will still be your bastard. I won't let him suffer that, Marco. I'm going home.'

'Niroli is my child's home, and this is where you and he are staying. When did you find out—about the child?' he demanded abruptly.

'Very recently. I had no idea...' Emily looked away from

Marco, remembering how shocked she had been. 'I would never have agreed to come here with you, if I'd known.'

'So how would you have informed me that I'd become a father? Via a birth notice in *The Times*?'

Emily flinched as she heard the savagery in his voice. 'That wouldn't happen,' she told him quietly. It had been foolish of her to give in to her urge to comfort him, because now she had created a new set of problems. Why had she told him? Because secretly she had been hoping—what? That he would sweep her up into his arms and say that he was thrilled she was expecting their child?

'I'm sorry if I've given you a shock. I was stunned myself when I realised. But I didn't want you to think I was leaving because…' The words 'because I don't love you' formed a tight knot that blocked her throat. How could she say them when she knew he didn't want her love? 'I wanted you to know that I have a valid reason for leaving the island,' she amended, her voice growing firmer as she underlined, 'a reason that matters to both of us. We already knew that one day we would have to part. The fact that I have accidentally conceived your child only makes that parting all the more essential. We both know that. I will not be your pregnant mistress, Marco.'

Emily was having his child, their child! A complex mixture of unfamiliar emotions were curling their fingers into his heart and tugging hard on it.

'How far advanced is this pregnancy?' he asked her brusquely.

Emily felt as though her whole body had been plunged into ice-cold water. This was what she had dreaded. An argument with him, in which he would try to demand that she terminate her pregnancy—something she had absolutely no intention of doing.

'I'm not sure,' she admitted honestly. 'I think that possibly it could have happened when I had that stomach bug. I remember reading somewhere that that kind of thing can neutralise the effect of the contraceptive pill. I should have thought about that at the time, but I didn't.' She lifted her head and told him firmly, '*You* needn't worry about the consequences, though, Marco. I am fully prepared to take sole responsibility for my child.'

'My child.' Marco stopped her ruthlessly. 'The child is my child, Emily.'

She looked at him uncertainly. It hadn't occurred to her that he would react like this. He sounded almost as though he felt as possessive about the baby as she did herself.

'I don't want to discuss it any more, Marco. There's no point. I can't stay here now.'

The morning sun was slanting across the courtyard. The coffee Maria had brought him half an hour earlier had grown cold as Marco sat deep in thought. He was not going to let Emily leave. And he was not going to allow his child to grow up anywhere other than here on Niroli. Both were unassailable and unchangeable tenets of what he felt about his role as king-in-waiting and as the father of Emily's expected baby. It wasn't any longer a matter of what he did or didn't want; it was a matter of his royal duty, to his pride, to his name and to his first-born.

It was ridiculous of Emily to suggest that their child would have benefits that his so-called legitimate children would not, folly for her to claim that he would one day thank her for denying him his royal status. Marco might have enjoyed the freedom of his time in London, but he had also never forgotten who and what he was. Having royal blood and being able to lay claim to it, even if one was born on the wrong side of the blanket, was a life-enhancing benefit that couldn't be ignored. His son, growing up here on Niroli as his accepted child, could look forward to the best of everything and, when grown, a position of authority at his father's court. He would be revered and respected, he would wield power and he would be on hand to support his legitimate half-sibling when finally he became King. Would he be imprisoned by his royal status, as Marco had sometimes felt he had been? No!

All of that and more could be made possible for this child, provided that Emily was prepared to see sense. She didn't have the status of a proper royal mistress, that was true. But his grandfather, for all his faults and stubbornness, also had a strong sense of duty and family. He, too, would want his great-grandchild to remain on Niroli. There was a way in which it could be made possible for her to stay and be elevated to a position in which she and their baby would have the respect of the people.

He swung round as he heard Emily come out into the court-yard. The sun had brushed her skin a warm gold, driving away its London pallor. She wasn't showing any visible sign of her pregnancy yet, but there was a rich glow about her, somehow, a sense of ripeness to come. Watching her, Marco experienced a swift surge of possessive determination not to let her go. She was having his child; whether by accident and not by design, that did not alter his paternal responsibilities or that a baby of royal blood was to be born. Who other than he could tell that child about his heritage and where better a place to do that than here on Niroli?

'I've just seen Maria and she's going to bring out some fresh coffee for you.' How domestic and comfortable that sounded, Emily thought tiredly as she sat down on the chair Marco had pulled out for her. She had hardly slept, her thoughts circling helplessly and tumultuously.

'I'm not prepared to let you leave the island, Emily. You,

and my child, are going to stay here where both of you belong. It seems to me that marriage is the best way to secure our son's future and your position at court.'

Marriage! Emily almost dropped the glass of water she had been drinking. Marco wanted to marry her? She was shaking from head to foot with the intensity of her joy. Emotional tears filled her eyes. She put down the glass, and protested shakily, 'Marco! You can't mean that. How can you marry me?'

She realised immediately from his expression that something was wrong.

'I can't marry you,' he told her flatly. 'You know that. What on earth made you think that I could?' Why did he feel this dragging weight wrapping itself around him? He couldn't marry Emily, and he was surprised that she had thought he might. And, yet, just for a moment, seeing the joy in her eyes, he had felt… He had felt *what?* A reciprocal surge of joy within himself? That was ridiculous.

'You need a husband, Emily, and a position at court. There is within European royal families a tradition whereby noblemen close to the throne marry royal mistresses. This kind of marriage is rather like a business arrangement, in that it benefits all parties and, in the eyes of the world, bestows respectability on the mistress and any children she may bear. The nobleman in question is of course rewarded for his role and—'

'Stop it. Stop it. I have heard enough!' Emily had pushed back her chair and got to her feet. She could hardly breathe but she struggled to speak. 'I thought I knew you, Marco. I even felt sorry for you, because of the heavy responsibility your duty to the Crown lays upon you! But now I realise that I never really knew you. The man I thought I knew would never in a thousand years have allowed himself to become so corrupted by power and pride that he would suggest what you have just suggested to me!'

'What I propose is a traditional solution to a uniquely royal problem,' Marco persisted curtly. 'You are overreacting.' Her outburst had made him feel as though he were doing something wrong, instead of recommending a logical solution to their problem. A logical solution of the kind his grandfather would have suggested? Was the pressure of becoming King turning him into a man like his grandfathe, the kind of man he had once sworn he would never allow himself to be? His critical inner voice would not be silenced, and its contempt echoed uncomfortably inside him.

'Am I? Take a look at yourself, Marco, and try seeing yourself through my eyes, and then repeat what you have just offered as a solution. You want to bribe another man to marry me so that—so that *what?* You can have your child here, conveniently legitimised by a convenient marriage between two strangers, though I'm sure that won't stop the gossip. But what about me? Am I expected to be a dutiful bride to this noble husband you're going to find for me? Am I supposed to submit willingly to having sex with him, bear his children, be his wife in all senses of the word?'

'No, there will be no question of that.' The harshness of his own immediate denial caught Marco off guard. But he couldn't retract his words, nor deny the feeling of fierce possessiveness that had gripped him at the thought of Emily in another man's bed.

'What kind of man are you, Marco, if you think that I would be willing to sell myself into such an arrangement? But then I was forgetting: you aren't a mere man, are you? You are a king! I'm not staying on the island a minute longer than I have to. Everything you've just said underlines all the reasons why I don't want my son growing up here. Your proximity to the throne has corrupted you, but I don't intend to let it corrupt my child.'

'And I don't intend to let you leave Niroli.'

They had been the closest of lovers, but now they were enemies locked in a battle to the bitter end for the right to decide the future of their child.

CHAPTER THIRTEEN

THE plane had taken off, but Emily was holding her breath, half expecting that, somehow, Marco still could prevent her from leaving Niroli.

She'd hated having to appeal to Marco's grandfather for help behind his back. At first, the king had refused to see her when she'd made her secret visit to the palace. She had been expecting his rejection, though, and so had lifted her chin and told the stiff-faced, uniformed equerry who had told her that the king would not receive her, 'Please tell His Majesty that the favour I want to ask him will benefit both of us and the throne of Niroli.'

She had been made to wait over an hour before she had finally been shown into the royal presence. It had shocked her to see how very like the king Marco was, traces of Marco's stunning good looks still visible in the older man's profile.

She had chosen her moment with care, waiting until she knew that Marco had gone up to the mountains to see Rafael before she visited the palace.

'I want to leave Niroli,' she told King Giorgio. 'But Marco does not wish me to leave. He has said he will do everything in his power to stop me and to keep me here.' She didn't tell the king about her pregnancy, just in case he echoed Marco's insistence that her child be brought up under the cover of an arranged marriage between herself and a nobleman.

'Only you have the authority to enable me to leave without Marco knowing.'

'Why should I do that?' the king challenged her.

Emily was ready for that. 'Because you do not want me here,' she replied. 'You do not consider me good enough to be Marco's mistress.'

'He is not the man I thought if he cannot provide sufficient inducement to keep you in his bed, if that is where he wants you.'

'Marco is more than man enough for any woman,' Emily defended. 'But I am too much of a woman to be prepared to share him with the throne and everything else that entails.'

She thought she saw a glimmer of grudging respect in the king's eyes before he gave a stiff nod of his head. 'Very well. I will help you. A royal flight will be made ready for you, and I shall ensure that Marco is kept out of the way until it has taken off.'

The king had kept his promise to her, and now she was on her way home. She closed her eyes against the acid burn of her tears and pressed her hand against her body as though in mute apology to her baby for what she was doing. 'You may not understand it now, but I'm doing this for you and for your future,' she whispered to him.

'How dare you do this?' White-faced with rage, Marco towered over his grandfather, royal protocol forgotten in his fury. Now he knew why Rafael had kept him at the village for so long with his endless complaints against young Tomasso and his friends.

When he had returned to the villa to find Emily missing, he had summoned Maria, and she had been the one who had told him that a car bearing the royal crest had arrived for her.

He had gone straight to the palace, demanding to see his grandfather.

'Emily applied to me for aid, because she feared you would force her to remain here on Niroli against her will. Naturally, I helped her.'

'Naturally,' Marco agreed grimly, registering even more grimly that her departure had elevated Emily from being a floozy to someone his grandfather was prepared to speak of with far more intimacy. 'After all, you never wanted her here.'

'Whatever role she might have played in your life in London, there is no place for her here on Niroli. She herself accepts this and, in doing so, she shows far more sense and awareness of the importance of your future role than you do, Marco. I confess that she impressed me with her grasp of your responsibility. She fully understands what will entail when you become Niroli's king.'

'She also fully understands that she is to be the mother of my child,' Marco told his grandfather sharply. 'That is why she has left—but I don't expect she told you that, did she?'

'She is having your child?'

'Yes,' Marco confirmed unashamedly.

The king was frowning imperiously. 'But that alters everything. Why did you not say something to me about this? She must be brought back, and at once! What if this child she is carrying should be a son? It is unthinkable that he should be brought up anywhere but here. Sons are a precious commodity, Marco, even if they are illegitimate. It is important that this child grows up on Niroli knowing his duty and his responsibility to the Crown. That knowledge cannot be instilled in him too early. When is the birth expected? There is much to do—the royal nursery will have to be prepared, and a suitable household established to take charge of him. The mother can stay in London if she wishes, in fact it would be better if she did,' the king continued dismissively.

His grandfather was only painting a picture that was similar to the one he himself had put before Emily. But instead of feeling vindicated, Marco could feel a cold heaviness seeping through him, as though leaden weights had been tied to his hands so that he was effectively imprisoned.

'You will order the woman to return, and when you do you will inform her that it is against the law of Niroli for anyone to remove a child of royal blood from the island, on penalty of death.'

Marco shook his head.

'Don't be ridiculous, Grandfather. Once in some mediae-val age it might have been possible to make such a threat, but I can tell you now that the British courts will take a dim view of it, and that Emily is totally within her rights to want to keep her child with her. I would certainly support her in that. I want my child to grow up here, yes, but I also want his mother to be here for him, as well.'

'Ridiculous sentimentality. I blame your mother for it. And your father. He should have insisted that she followed tradi-tion and handed you over to those appointed to be responsible for your care as a future king, instead of meddling in matters that did not concern her. It is thanks to her that you developed this stubborn streak that puts you at odds with your duty.'

Marco forced himself not to say anything. Instead he focused on his childhood. He could see himself playing, running and his mother chasing him, and he could see too the disapproving looks of the elderly courtiers his grandfather had insisted were to be responsible for his upbringing and forma-tion. His mother, had she still been alive, would have sup-ported Emily and helped her. They would have got on well. His father had struggled to oppose the king's insistence that Marco was brought up to be a prince, rather than as a member of a warm and loving family. His grandfather would try to impose his will on his great-grandchild, Marco knew. He frowned, suddenly sharply aware of his own desire to protect his child from the cold discipline and royal training he had known in his own childhood. He was not his father, he reminded himself. He was more than strong enough to ensure that his son was not subjected to the misery of his boyhood.

'Whilst you are here,' his grandfather was continuing imperiously, 'I have decided that the generators will have to be removed from the island completely. They are causing too much conflict between our peoples. It is just as I had thought, these young dissidents in the mountains have been encouraged by the Viallis to band together and challenge the authority of their village elders. And the blame for that can be laid at our door, Marco. By publicly going against my wishes, you have turned yourself into a figurehead for their rebellion. Various informants have told me of their concern that they are only waiting until you are on the throne to force your hand and make demands that can never be granted. If there is any more trouble, I shall impose a curfew—that will teach them to respect the law and the Crown.'

'If these youngsters are angry and filled with resentment, who can blame them?' Marco demanded. 'They need the controls on their lives relaxing, not tightening to the point where there is bound to be increased conflict. By imposing a curfew, all you will be doing is driving their feelings underground and alienating them further. What we need is to establish a forum in which they feel they can be heard and their views properly addressed.'

'What, reward them for their rebelliousness and their disrespect? They need teaching a lesson, not to be indulged.'

'Have a care, Grandfather,' Marco warned. 'Feed their sense of injustice by imposing your royal will, and in the end we will all pay a heavy price.'

'Bah…! You are too soft, too much the modern liberal. You cannot rule Niroli like that, Marco. You rule it like this!' The old king closed his fist and banged it down hard on the table in front of him. 'By letting them know what it is to fear your anger.'

As he had learned to fear his grandfather's anger as a child? As his son would be forced to learn to fear it? Marco was filled with a sense of revulsion. He had returned to Niroli committed to working to improve things for its people, but now he was beginning to question his ability to do that. With his grandfather so opposed to the changes he wanted to make, and his own views so diametrically opposed to the king's, weren't they more likely to tear Niroli apart between them than anything else? Perhaps Emily was right to refuse to allow their child to be brought up here?

Marco closed his eyes, deep in thought. No, his son should be here because he, his father, was here. Emily would have to accept his determination to play his royal role, whether she liked it or not…

CHAPTER FOURTEEN

EMILY sat huddled in the squashy, cream-ticking-covered chair in the pretty sitting room of her Chelsea home, staring numbly at the letter she was holding. Not that she needed to read it again. She knew its every word off by heart, she had read it so many times since it had arrived two days ago: the consultant at the hospital where she had been for her twenty-week pregnancy scan wanted her to return, so that they could do a further test.

She had of course rung the hospital the moment she had received the summons, and the nurse she had spoken to had assured her that there was no need for her to worry. But Emily was very worried. In fact, she was worried sick, reliving over and over again that tell-tale moment during the ultrasound when the young operative had suddenly hesitated and then looked uncertainly at Emily before carrying on. Nothing had been said; she knew the scan had shown that her baby had all the right number of fingers and toes, and had even confirmed her belief that she was carrying Marco's son. If she hadn't received the letter requesting her to go back, she suspected she would never have given the girl's hesitation another thought. Why had she hesitated? Was there something wrong with her baby? Oh, please, God, don't let there be! Was she being punished because of what she had done? Because she had left Niroli? Because she was deliberately planning to lock Marco out of their son's life?

But that was to protect the baby, not punish Marco, she protested to herself.

The sound of someone ringing her doorbell brought her out of her painful thoughts: it would be Jemma. The shock of being requested to return for a second scan had brought home to her how alone in the world she was, and upset her so much that she had unburdened herself to her friend and assistant. As a result, Jemma had started to adopt an almost maternal attitude towards her and had insisted she would accompany her to her repeat scan. Smoothing down the skirt of the loose linen dress she was wearing, Emily got up to answer the door. Whilst she had been on Niroli a heatwave had come to the city and, at first, when she opened the door the light pouring in from the fashionable London street outside dazzled her so much that she thought she must be imagining things: it couldn't possibly be Marco who was standing on her immaculate doorstep, the formality of his dark business suit a perfect foil for the bright red of the geraniums that filled the elegant containers that flanked the entrance.

But it *was* Marco, and he was stepping into her hallway and closing the door behind him, looking just as impressive against the interior's old-English-white walls as he had done outside.

For a while after her return from Niroli, she had barely slept for fear that he would come after her and demand she go back. But there had been no sign of him. Then, the arrival of the letter had given her something much more worrying to keep her awake at night. Her heart was thumping in jerky uncoordinated beats; he had brought with him in the hallway, not just his presence, but also his scent. Helpless tears of longing pricked in her eyes, blurring her vision.

'Is this what you're planning to take to the hospital?' Without waiting for her response, Marco leaned down to pick up the pale straw basket into which she had packed everything she thought she might need.

'The hospital?' Her voice faltered she was shocked by those words, her face nearly as pale as her hall walls.

'I've just been round to the shop. Jemma told me about the scan. I've got a cab waiting. Where are your keys?'

'Marco, there's no need for this. Jemma's coming with me.'

'No, she's not. *I* am going with you—there is every need for me to do so. This is my child you are carrying, Emily. Are you ready?'

She shouldn't be letting him take charge like this, Emily told herself, but the stress of the last few days was telling on her and she simply felt too weak and drained to argue with him. And, besides…if she was honest, wasn't there something comfortingly bitter-sweet about having him here with her…with them… Her hand went to her tummy as inwardly she whispered comforting words to her baby, promising it that, no matter what the scan showed, no matter what anyone said, he would have life and she would love him.

The stress of worrying about the baby had stolen from Emily the bloom she had gained whilst she'd been on Niroli, Marco recognised as he took hold of her arm and guided her to the waiting taxi.

Marco gave the driver the name of a private hospital, ignoring Emily's small start of surprise. It hadn't been difficult getting Jemma to tell him what had happened. In fact she had been so relieved to see him that she had told him everything he needed to know without him having to probe. He had come to London with the sole intention of taking Emily back to Niroli with him, and of telling her that their child would be born on the island and would remain there; whether or not she chose to do the same was up to her. Since he had last seen her, his feelings towards Emily had turned both angry and hostile. She had gone behind his back to his grandfather; she had walked out on him, she had insulted him. She'd given him, for no good reason whatsoever, sleepless nights analysing what she'd said and what she hadn't, trying to find ways he could fit together the pieces of the jigsaw his life now was, working out what would make it possible for him to have her living on Niroli with him—and willingly. And then going over everything he had already analysed once more, to double-check that the reason he wanted her there was only because of his child. Because, somehow, though he found it hard to admit, deep down inside, a suspicion still lurked that he wanted *Emily*.

But the news Jemma had given him about Emily being called back for a second scan had caused a seismic emotional shift within him, so that all he could think about now, all that concerned him and occupied his thoughts, was Emily and their baby.

The hospital was one of London's most exclusive and private and Emily's obstetrician had been likely recommended to her. He was a charming middle-aged man, with a reassuring smile and a taste for bow ties. In his letter, he had stated that he would be on hand once Emily had had her repeat scan to discuss the results. It made her feel sickly cold inside every time she thought about the underlying hint that there might be some kind of problem.

'Has anyone said why you are having to have a second scan?' Marco asked her as the taxi pulled up outside the hospital.

Emily shook her head.

'But you have asked?'

'I rang Mr Bryant-Jones, my obstetrician, and he said that sometimes a repeat scan was needed.'

'But he didn't explain why?'

'No,' Emily admitted shakily. Marco's terse words, along with his grim expression, were increasing her fear.

Marco paid the taxi driver and, still carrying her basket, put his free hand under her elbow, for all the world as protective as though he were a committed husband. But he wasn't, and Emily knew she must not give in to her longing to turn to him and get him to reassure her that she had no need to worry, and that everything was going to be all right.

The hospital's reception area could well have been that of an expensive hotel, Emily recognised, looking at the two receptionists who were stunningly attractive and very smartly dressed.

It was Marco, and not she, who stepped forward and gave her name. But any thought she had of objecting to his high-handed manner or to his taking charge disappeared when she heard him telling the receptionist very firmly, 'Please inform Emily's obstetrician, Mr Bryant-Jones, that we are here.'

'My appointment with him isn't until after I've had my scan,' Emily reminded Marco. She could see that he was about to say something, but before he could do so a smiling nurse came up to them, asking, 'Emily? We're ready for you now, if you'd like to come this way.'

'I shall be coming with her,' Marco informed the nurse imperiously.

'Yes, of course. It's this way,' the nurse replied pleasantly.

'This isn't where I had my last scan,' Emily commented anxiously.

'No. Mr Bryant-Jones has requested a three-D scan this time.'

'A three-D scan—what's that?' Emily asked apprehensively.

'Nothing to worry about,' the nurse reassured her cheerfully. 'It's just a special imaging process that gives us a clearer, more in-depth picture of the baby, that's all.'

'But why...I mean, why do you need that?'

Emily wasn't aware that she had stopped walking until she felt Marco reach out and take hold of her hand. Anxiously she looked up at him, mutely telling him that she didn't feel able to go any further.

'Here we are,' the nurse announced, opening a door several yards up the corridor and holding it open, waiting for Marco and Emily to catch up with her. 'I'll hand you over to Merle, now,' she told Emily as another nurse came forward to direct her over to the waiting bed.

'Once you've put on your gown, the ultrasonographer will start the scan. I'll be putting some gel on your tummy, like the last time,' she told Emily kindly.

'You don't need to be here for this, Marco,' Emily told Marco firmly as she pulled the curtains round the bed and got undressed. For once, the thought of the potential indignity of wearing the universal hospital gown, with its open back fastening, didn't bother her. All she could think about was her baby. Why wouldn't anyone tell her anything? Part of her was relieved that Marco was ignoring her request and not making any move to leave, but another part of her felt even more anxious. If there was something wrong with their baby, Marco's pride... It didn't matter what Marco thought. She would have her baby, no matter what.

When Emily had changed into her gown and she drew back the curtains, she looked both vulnerable and afraid. Just looking at her caused a sensation in Marco that felt like a giant fist squeezing his heart and wringing from it an emotion so concentrated that it burned his soul.

The nurse helped Emily lie down on the bed next to the scanner and covered her legs with a blanket, then she started applying the necessary gel.

Given she was around twenty weeks pregnant, her stomach was only gently rounded. Emily held her breath anxiously as the ultrasonographer, a very professional-looking young woman passed, the probe over her bump, whilst studying the resulting images on the screen in front on her.

'Why am I having to have this kind of scan?' Emily asked her.

'See—look, your baby is yawning.' The ultrasonographer smiled, ignoring her questions. Emily stared at the screen, her heart giving a fierce kick of awed joy as she stared avidly at the small but perfect form.

'Maybe he's not a he, but a she.'

Emily had been so engrossed in watching the screen that she hadn't realised that Marco had come to stand behind her and was looking over her head at the image of their baby.

'Oh, I think we can safely say that he is a he,' the girl told him with a broad smile and pointing, before suddenly going silent as she moved the scanner further up the baby's body. Then her smile gave way to a frown of concentration.

Why wasn't she saying anything? Emily worried. Why was she staring at the screen so intently? Her heart thumped with fear.

'What is it?' Emily asked anxiously. 'Is something wrong?'

'I'm almost finished and then you'll be able to go and get dressed,' the girl told her smoothly. 'You've got an appointment to see Mr Bryant-Jones, I think?'

'Yes,' Emily confirmed. 'Look, if there's something wrong with my baby…'

'Mr Bryant-Jones will discuss the scan with you.' The girl was using her professional mask to hold her at a distance, Emily recognised shakily. She looked at Marco. She could see in his eyes that he too was aware of the heavy weight of what the girl had not said hanging in the room. What was it? What was wrong? The tiny being she'd seen on the scan had been yawning and stretching—to her eye, he looked completely perfect. Maybe she was worrying unnecessarily. Maybe this *was* just a routine check.

Her fingers trembled as she re-dressed herself. On the other side of the curtain, she could hear Merle, the nurse, telling Marco that as soon as Emily was ready she would escort them down to see the obstetrician…

CHAPTER FIFTEEN

EMILY could feel her anxiety bathing her skin in perspiration as they were shown into the obstetrician's office. Mr Bryant-Jones was smiling, but not as widely as he had done the first time she had seen him.

'Ah, Emily, good. Good.' He was looking past her towards Marco, but before Emily could introduce him Marco stepped forward, extending his hand and saying curtly, 'Prince Marco of Niroli. I am the baby's father.'

'Ah. Yes…. Excellent.'

'Mr Bryant-Jones, why have I had to have another scan?' Emily demanded, unable to wait any longer. 'And this three-D scan, what is that—? Why…?'

'Please sit down, both of you.' The obstetrician wasn't smiling any more. He was looking at the scanned images he had on his desk, moving them around. 'I'm sorry to have to tell you this, but it looks as though your baby may have a heart defect.'

'A heart defect? What exactly does that mean? Will my baby—?' Emily couldn't get any further; her pent-up emotions were bursting out and making it impossible for her to speak.

'The baby will have to be between twenty-two to twenty-four weeks before we can make a full diagnosis. At this stage, all we can tell from the scans is that there is a likelihood that your baby could have a foetal heart abnormality.'

'You said there *could* be a heart abnormality.'

Marco's voice seemed to be reaching Emily from over a great distance, as though she weren't really here and taking part in this dreadful, dreadful scene, as though she and her baby had gone away somewhere private and safe where nothing bad could touch them.

'What exactly does that mean?' Marco questioned the obstetrician.

'It means that the baby's heart does not seem to be forming as it should. Now, this can be a small problem, or it can be a far more serious one. We cannot tell which, as yet. That is why you will need to see a cardiac specialist. There is a very good one here in this hospital, who collaborates with our specialist neo-natal unit. My recommendation would be that we arrange for you to visit him as soon as it can be arranged.'

'Is…is my baby going to die?' Emily's voice shook with fear.

'No,' the obstetrician assured her. 'But depending on how severe the abnormality is, there could be a series of operations throughout his childhood and teenage years and, maybe, if things are extreme, there will be the necessity for a heart transplant at some stage. Severe heart malfunctions do limit the kind of life the sufferer can live. If this is the case, your son will need dedicated care; boys like to run and play vigorous games, but it might be a possibility that he'll not be able to do that.'

Her child could be a boy who might not be able to run and play like other children, a boy who could be subjected to operation after operation to keep him alive! But he would have a life, and she would give every hour, every second, of her life to him and his needs, Emily vowed fiercely.

Marco looked across at Emily; he could see the devastation in her eyes. He wanted, he realised, to take her in his arms and hold her there. He wanted to tell her that there was nothing to fear and that he would keep both of them safe, her and their child. He wanted to tell her that he was there for them whatever happened and he always would be, and that they were the most, the only, important things in his life. The news they had just received had at a stroke filled him with an emotion so complex and yet so simple that it could not be denied.

Love…

What he was feeling for Emily right now was love: a man's love for his woman, the mother of his child, for his companion and soul mate, without whom his life would never be complete.

Earlier, while watching the scan take place, he had experienced the most extraordinary sense of enlightenment, of knowing that he had to be part of his son's life. Now had come the knowledge that nothing could ever be more important to him than guarding this precious, growing life and the woman who was carrying it.

Not power, not wealth, nothing; not even the throne of Niroli.

Marco knew that others would not understand; he barely understood what he was experiencing himself. But, somehow, it wasn't necessary for him to understand, or to be able to analyse; it was simply enough for him to know. Maybe he had been travelling towards this place, this cross-roads in his life, for longer than he realised; maybe there had been many signposts along the journey that he had not seen. However, now, not only had the crossroads been reached, they had been traversed simply and easily, without any kind of hesitation or doubt. He could not be Niroli's king *and* his child's father—certainly not this child's father, whose young life might always hang precariously on a thread, and who should never be subjected to the rigours of kingship. This boy would need his father's loving presence. And he would have it. Singularly, neither he nor Emily was strong enough for their child, but together they would be.

'I have to return to Niroli.'

They were back home in Emily's kitchen. The necessary appointment had been made with the cardiac specialist, and now Emily inclined her head slightly as she listened to Marco.

'Yes, of course,' she agreed. She had been expecting him to say this, and she knew, too, that there would be no demands from him now that she should return with him so that his son could grow up on the island. The royal family of Niroli were arrogant and proud, too arrogant and proud to want to accept that one of their bloodline could be anything less than perfect. No, Marco would not want a sickly, ailing child around to remind him of that. She could feel the pain of the rejection on behalf of her baby, but she stifled it. It was Marco who was not worthy of their child, not the other way around. Not worthy of her child and not worthy of her love.

Marco desperately wanted to tell Emily how he felt—but this was not the right time. Unfortunately, he had a duty to inform his grandfather first of his intentions. Once he had done that, then he could tell Emily how much he loved her. Did she love him? His heart felt as though there were a knife twisting inside it. But even if she didn't love him, he still intended to be a full-time father to his son.

'I'll be back in time for the appointment with the cardiac specialist.'

Emily bowed her head. She mustn't let her own feelings swamp her. She had to be strong—for her son. Was it something she had done, or not done, that had caused his heart defect? she had asked the obstetrician.

No, Mr Bryant-Jones had told her, sometimes the condition ran in families, but sometimes it 'just happened', without there being any reason.

'What do you mean you no longer wish to succeed to the throne?'

'I mean, Grandfather, that I am abdicating my claim to the Crown. I intend to make a formal speech to that effect, but I wanted you to be the first to know,' Marco told his grandfather calmly.

'You are giving up the throne of Niroli for the sake of a woman and her child.'

Marco could hear the disbelief in his grandfather's voice.

'*My* woman and *my* child. And, yes, I am giving up the throne for them. For them, and for our people.'

'What do you mean by that?'

'It would never have worked, Grandfather. I could never step into your shoes.' Marco saw that the old man was looking slightly gratified.

'For me, they would be constraining, too limiting,' he finished firmly. 'We have done nothing but argue since I first arrived. You block every attempt I make to make reforms—'

'Because they are not right for our people.'

'No, because they are not right for you.'

'What you want to do would cause a schism that would split the island.'

'If you continued to oppose me, then, yes, there is that possibility. Niroli needs a king who will bring it into the twenty-first century—I firmly believe that. But I also believe now that Niroli's king can never be me. That does not mean that I don't care about my homeland and my people, I do—passionately—but I now know that I can do more for it and for them by working from outside its hierarchy.'

'By spreading anarchy, you mean?'

'By setting up a charitable trust to help those who most need it,' Marco corrected him evenly.

There was a certain irony in the fact that, whilst he had refused to wear the heavily decorated formal uniform his grandfather had had made for him on his arrival in Niroli, he was wearing it now to take his formal leave, Marco admitted as he waited for the king's equally elderly valet to finish fastening him into the jacket with its heavy gold braid. But somehow it seemed fitting that, on this one occasion, he should defer to tradition.

The world's media had been alerted to the fact that he intended to make a public speech; TV and radio crews had already arrived and the square below the palace balcony, from which he had chosen to address the people, was already full.

How different he felt now, compared with the way he had felt when he had first returned. Then, he had been filled with a fierce determination to fulfil his destiny; it had ridden him and possessed him.

This morning he had woken up with a sense of release, a sense of having gained back a part of himself he was only just becoming aware he had been denying.

The valet handed him his plumed hat. He could hear the shrill sound of trumpets. Walking slowly and majestically, he headed for the balcony, timing his entrance to when the military band broke into the Nirolian national anthem. Then he stepped forward…

CHAPTER SIXTEEN

EMILY stopped outside A shop window to look at her reflection and push her hair off her face. It was a sullenly hot day and her back was aching. She had been to see a client, but had hardly been able to focus on what the man had been saying to her because of her dread of what the cardiac specialist might say. Part of her wanted to rush the appointment and the specialist's opinion of her baby's future forward, whilst another part of her wanted to push it away. She was standing outside an electrical store that sold televisions. Its windows were filled with a variety of large screens. She glanced absently at them and then froze in disbelief when she realised she was looking at Marco. A camera homed in on his face, and then panned to the crowd in the square beneath him.

What was happening? Emily could think of only one thing: Marco must already be formally taking his position as the new King of Niroli. She wanted to ignore the screens and walk on past the shop, but instead she found that she was going inside.

'This is a most extraordinary event,' she could hear a TV news commentator saying excitedly. 'The royal family of Niroli is one of the richest in the world. They live according to their own set of rules. Of course the current King of Niroli is Giorgio. However, there have been rumours for some time that he is about to step down in favour of his grandson, Prince Marco. Now we have learned that Prince Marco has said that there is something he wants to tell his people. It can only mean one thing. What a change this will be for the island. There are already mutterings that Prince Marco wants to make too many changes too quickly, and that these could stir up unrest…'

Whilst the commentator talked over the last notes of the Nirolian national anthem, Emily focused feverishly on Marco's face. This could be the last time she would ever see him.

'People of Niroli…' he said in Italian. Tears stung Emily's eyes as she read the English subtitles at the bottom of the screen. She could hear the strength of purpose in Marco's voice as he went on, 'What I have to tell you today causes me great joy and also great sadness. Great joy, because when I leave you I shall be making the most important commitment a man ever can make, a commitment to the future through the next generation. Great sadness, because, in order to do that, I must abdicate my responsibility to you, the people of Niroli—'

Emily could almost feel the ripple of shock surging through the listening crowd. Her own thoughts were in turmoil. What was Marco doing? What was he saying? He was Niroli's future king and nothing could or should change that… She had listened to his passionate diatribes against his grandfather and she had known his fierce longing to do something to help his people. And yet now he was saying…

Marco was still speaking, so she moved closer to the screen.

'It is my belief that Niroli and its people need a ruler with a different mindset from my own, a ruler who can combine the best of the old ways with a new path into the twenty-first century. I am not that man, as both my grandfather and I have agreed. King Giorgio needs an heir to step into his shoes whom he can trust to preserve all that is good in our traditions.

Niroli also needs a new king who can take it forward into the future. With the best will in the world, I cannot be that king.'

A low murmur of objection filled the air accompanied by younger male voices shouting angrily and declaring, according to the TV commentator, that Marco was the king they wanted. Tomasso and his friends, Emily guessed.

'Do not think, though, my people, that I am deserting you, for I am not. I am soon to be the father of a child, and that knowledge has taught me how important the bond is between parent and child, between generation and generation, between a ruler and his people. My love for my child fills me and humbles me, and reinforces in me my love for the people of Niroli. It is out of this love—both for my child and for you, my people—that I am stepping down from the succession line to the throne, but never think that I am deserting you. I intend to set up a charity which will make available funds to help those citizens of Niroli who are most in need. It will provide the opportunity for our young people to be educated and to travel abroad, to broaden their horizons and then bring back to Niroli the gift of what they have learned so that they may share it. It is my passionate belief that this island needs a better system for encouraging its young to reach their full potential. I can do this best from outside the hierarchy of kingship and all that goes with it. At the same time, I shall remain at all times supportive of my grandfather and whoever he chooses to take the throne after him.

'I ask for your blessing, people of Niroli, and your understanding that sometimes it is more important for a man to be just that, than for him to be a king…'

'Excuse me, love, only we're about to close the store.' Her gaze blurred with her tears, Emily looked at the young man who was addressing her. Marco had left the balcony. The young man was looking impatient. Reluc-tantly, she nodded her head and headed for the exit.

It wasn't a long walk from the shops back to her house, but it was long enough for Emily to mentally question what Marco had done. He had told his people that he was giving up the throne because of his child—her child. Why? Marco was arrogant and proud, a perfectionist; did he—or his grandfather—fear the exis- tence of a child who was not perfect might somehow damage the power of the Nirolian royal family? Had his grandfather pressured Marco into stepping down, or had his own resolve spurred his abdication? Either way, she had no wish to be a party to depriving Niroli of its future king, and nor did she want her son growing up carrying the burden and the blame for his father's decision to deny himself a role Emily knew he had been eager to take on.

She turned the corner into her street and then stopped, her heart hammering against her ribs as she saw Marco standing outside the front door of her house. Ridiculously, her first impulse was to turn and walk away, but he had already seen her and he was walking towards her.

'What are you doing here?' she demanded when he reached her. 'I've only just seen you on television! Marco, you can't give up the Crown. Why have you? It isn't—'

'It isn't your decision,' Marco told her calmly. 'It was mine, and as for you seeing me on TV, well, it must have been on a rolling news programme rounding up the day's events. I made my resignation speech at eleven a.m. this morning, Nirolian time. I had a private jet standing by, another personal decision, before you ask,' he added dryly.

'It isn't fair of you to do this and to say publicly that it's because of my baby,' she told him passionately. 'Isn't he going to have enough to cope with, without the added blame of being responsible for—'

'We can't discuss this out here,' Marco interrupted her. 'Where are your keys?'

Helplessly, Emily handed them over and let him open the door for her.

The small house smelled of Emily's delicate scent, Marco recognised, also realising how much he had missed her. Soon, no doubt, the air around her would be filled with the scent of baby powder. With every mile that had brought him closer to her, his conviction that he had made the right decision had grown and, now, recognising how much he was looking forward to being part of the family unit they would form with their child was like one door closing behind him on an old habitat that no longer had any relevance to his life and another opening that had everything to do with it.

'There was no need for you to abdicate, Marco,' Emily burst out as soon as they were inside. 'I know how much you wanted to be King, so why?'

'If you had heard my speech in its entirety, then you would have known why I decided to step down, and why it was necessary for me to abdicate.'

'Because of our baby? Because he might not be perfect? Because you're ashamed of him, and you and your grandfather don't want him associated with Niroli?'

'What? Ashamed of him? You wouldn't be more wrong. If there's anyone I'm ashamed of, it's myself for taking so long to recognise what really matters to me. Or perhaps I did recognise it, but tried to pretend that I didn't. Emily, when you were having your scan and I saw our baby, I knew beyond any kind of doubt that you and he are the most important things in the world to me, and that nothing could ever or would ever matter more. Actually, I think I knew a little of that when I first came to Niroli and I missed you so much I had to come back for you. I certainly knew it when you told me you were pregnant and all I could think of was finding a way to keep you with me. I couldn't and wouldn't accept that it wasn't possible for me to be King and to have you and our child. And then you told me why you were pleased that our child would never be King, and it was as though you had unlocked a door inside me. Behind it lay the memories of my own childhood, my parents' constant battles with my grandfather to provide me with a normal childhood, my own sense of aloneness because of what I was, and I knew unequivocally that you were right not to want that for our child.'

'But you wanted to be King! You had so many plans, there was so much you wanted to do—you can't give that up.'

'I don't intend to. I can still do all those things without being King. In fact I can do them more easily. My grandfather would never really release the reins of government to me, and the hostility between us and the constant fight for supremacy would not aid our people. I can do far more outside the constraints of kingship, and I can do those things with you at my side. I love you, Emily.'

There was so much she wanted to say, so many questions, so many reminders to him of times when he had not seemed to love her at all. But, somehow, she was in his arms and he was kissing her with a fierce, demanding passion that said more clearly than any amount of words what he truly felt.

'I still can't believe this is happening,' Emily whispered to Marco half an hour later. She was still in his arms, only now they were upstairs in her bedroom, lying side by side in her bed. The way Marco had controlled his need to possess her, been gentle to protect their child, had brought emotional tears to her eyes and flooded her heart with the love for him she had dammed up for so long.

'You want me to convince you?' Marco teased her suggestively, his hand cupping her breast.

'Maybe,' she agreed mock-demurely.

His, 'Right, come on then, let's get dressed,' wasn't the response she had been expecting and her chagrin showed, making him laugh.

'We're going shopping,' he told her. 'For a wedding ring and a marriage licence.'

When her eyes rounded, he pointed out, 'You said you wanted me to convince you. I can't think of a better way to do that than marrying you, just as soon as we can arrange it.'

'Oh, Marco... Shouldn't we wait to make plans until after the scan?'

'Why? The potential severity of our baby's heart defect doesn't make any difference to my feelings for you or for him. You suggested earlier that I might be ashamed of our baby for not being perfect. That could never happen. He will be perfect to me, Emily, because he is ours, perfect in every way, no matter what.'

'Oh, don't,' Emily protested. 'You'll make me cry all over again.'

'And then I'll have to kiss you all over again,' Marco said, pretending to give a weary sigh, but smiling whilst he did so.

'Well, then, let's have a look. It's been a few weeks since we did your last scan, and that will have given your baby a chance to grow and us the chance to get a better idea of what's going on. As I told you at your first consultation with me, these days, in-utero surgery means that we can do so very much more than we once could. Even with the most severe cases.'

Emily felt Marco squeezing her hand, but she dared not look at him just in case she broke down.

These last weeks since their initial appointment with the neo-natal heart consultant had seemed so long, despite the fact that they had managed to squeeze getting married into them, along with a flying visit to Niroli, where Marco's grandfather had very graciously welcomed her formally into the family. Marco had also brought his grandfather up to date with his plans to establish the charity he had promised during his abdication speech.

New scans had been done, and now they were waiting anxiously for the specialist's opinion.

'However, in the case of your baby, I don't consider that an operation would be appropriate.'

Emily gave a small moan of despair. Was he saying there was no hope? 'What exactly is our baby's prognosis?' Marco's voice wasn't quite as level as normal, and Emily could hear the uncertainty in it.

'Very good. Excellent, in fact,' the specialist told them, smiling. 'There is a small area that we shall need to keep an eye on, but if anything it seems to be healing itself—something we do see with this condition. Sometimes babies will grow in stops and starts, and this leads us to make diagnoses we later have to amend. That is what has happened here. Initially, it did look as though your baby's heart might not be developing properly, but these latest scans show that everything is just as it should be.'

'Are you sure?' Emily asked anxiously. 'I mean, should I have another scan in a week or two? What if—?'

'I am perfectly sure. In fact, I was pretty sure when you first came to see me, but I wanted to wait and see how things went before I said anything, which is why I wanted to do this last scan. Of course, I am going to recommend that we continue to monitor the situation, just to be on the safe side, but my view is that there is nothing for you to worry about. Your baby is perfectly healthy and developing normally.'

Outside on the street, oblivious to the amused looks of passers-by, Marco held Emily close and tenderly kissed the tears from her face.

'I can't believe it,' she whispered to him. 'Oh, Marco… It's like a miracle.'

'You are my miracle, Emily,' Marco told her softly. 'You and our child, and the future we are going to share.'

'How has the king taken things?'

'Not as badly as we might have feared.' The senior courtier was well versed in tact and diplomacy, and he had no intention of telling the junior aide anything about the extraordinary scene he had just witnessed in the Royal Chamber, when the king had stopped in mid-rant about the stupidity of his grandson and heir to stare at the report he had just been handed, about an Australian surgeon who was pioneering a new treatment for the heart condition from which the king himself suffered.

On the face of it, there had been nothing in the grainy photograph and short biography of the young Australian to cause such a reaction. But the senior courtier had been in service at the palace for a very long time and when the king had handed the report to him in an expectant silence he, too, had seen the same thing that the king had seen.

'I want that young man brought here, and I want him brought here now,' the king had instructed….

In the heart of the Arabian desert, a solitary figure surveys the kingdom he loves...

THIS was no ordinary sandstorm. It seemed that the air itself was sent to punish him. The fine crystals whipped at his eyes but he made no move to shield his face. He hadn't come here to shy away from the elements. He had come to embrace what was his, the land that for centuries had spoken his name, the kingdom that, from the very day he was born, was his for the taking. But why couldn't he hear it calling...?

Deeper, further, he pounded his way into the depths of the desert. His desert. The arid land burning his soles, the harsh wind pulling at his robes, at his hair, at his soul. But still he found nothing. The shadow on his jaw darkened as he strode through the night. The heavy lids over his eyes never once drooping in sleep, the fine beads of sweat trickling in a salty line over a body that was built for stamina, for grace, for danger. A body and a mind that could sense the upcoming battle he would face. A battle of duty and destiny. A battle that would take him from this kingdom, this home, to the place that lay in the very core of his being.

By morning he turned and faced directly to the sun, his

thick lashes shielding his eyes from the burning intensity. It was time to leave this place. This barren land had answered him. Taken him, and shown him the truth. And one corner of his mouth raised in a lazy gesture of understanding. The journey had only just begun…

* * * * *

*Find out more about this mystery desert prince
and where his journey will lead him in
SURGEON PRINCE, ORDINARY WIFE,
book two of* The Royal House of Niroli.

**He's proud, passionate, primal—
dare she surrender to the sheikh?**

Feel warm winds blowing through your hair and the
hot desert sun on your skin as you are transported to
exotic lands. As the temperature rises, let yourself be
seduced by our sexy, irresistible sheikhs.

If you love our men of the desert, look for more stories
in this enthralling miniseries coming soon!

Rosalie Winters doesn't engage in the games of flirtation
that Sheikh Arik expects from women—but once
Rosalie is under his command, she'll open up to receive
the loving that only he can give her.

FOR THE SHEIKH'S PLEASURE

by Annie West

Always passionate, always proud.

**The richest royal family in the world—
a family united by blood and passion,
torn apart by deceit and desire.**

By royal decree, Harlequin Presents is delighted to bring
you *The Royal House of Niroli*. Step into the glamorous,
enticing world of the Nirolian Royal Family. As the king
ails, he must find an heir...each month an exciting new
installment follows the epic search for the true Nirolian
king. Eight heirs, eight romances, eight fantastic stories!

Be sure not to miss any of the passion!

Coming in August:
SURGEON PRINCE, ORDINARY WIFE
by Melanie Milburne

When brilliant surgeon Dr. Alex Hunter discovers he's the missing
Prince of Niroli long thought dead, he is torn between duty and
his passion for Amelia Vialli, who can never be his queen....

Coming in September:
BOUGHT BY THE BILLIONAIRE PRINCE
by Carol Marinelli

REQUEST YOUR FREE BOOKS!

HARLEQUIN *Presents*®

2 FREE NOVELS PLUS 2 FREE GIFTS!

PASSION GUARANTEED SEDUCTION

YES! Please send me 2 FREE Harlequin Presents® novels and my 2 FREE gifts. After receiving them, if I don't wish to receive any more books, I can return the shipping statement marked "cancel." If I don't cancel, I will receive 6 brand-new novels every month and be billed just $3.80 per book in the U.S., or $4.47 per book in Canada, plus 25¢ shipping and handling per book and applicable taxes, if any*. That's a savings of close to 15% off the cover price! I understand that accepting the 2 free books and gifts places me under no obligation to buy anything. I can always return a shipment and cancel at any time. Even if I never buy another book from Harlequin, the two free books and gifts are mine to keep forever.

106 HDN EEXK   306 HDN EEXV

Name	(PLEASE PRINT)	
Address		Apt. #
City	State/Prov.	Zip/Postal Code

Signature (if under 18, a parent or guardian must sign)

Mail to the **Harlequin Reader Service®:**
IN U.S.A.: P.O. Box 1867, Buffalo, NY 14240-1867
IN CANADA: P.O. Box 609, Fort Erie, Ontario L2A 5X3

Not valid to current Harlequin Presents subscribers.

**Want to try two free books from another line?
Call 1-800-873-8635 or visit www.morefreebooks.com.**

* Terms and prices subject to change without notice. NY residents add applicable sales tax. Canadian residents will be charged applicable provincial taxes and GST. This offer is limited to one order per household. All orders subject to approval. Credit or debit balances in a customer's account(s) may be offset by any other outstanding balance owed by or to the customer. Please allow 4 to 6 weeks for delivery.

Your Privacy: Harlequin is committed to protecting your privacy. Our Privacy Policy is available online at www.eHarlequin.com or upon request from the Reader Service. From time to time we make our lists of customers available to reputable firms who may have a product or service of interest to you. If you would prefer we not share your name and address, please check here.

HP07

HARLEQUIN®

Mediterranean NIGHTS™

Glamour, elegance, mystery and revenge aboard the high seas...

Coming in August 2007...

THE TYCOON'S SON

by
award-winning author
Cindy Kirk

Businessman Theo Catomeris's long-estranged father is determined to reconnect with his son, so he hires Trish Melrose to persuade Theo to renew his contract with Liberty Line. Sailing aboard the luxurious *Alexandra's Dream* is a rare opportunity for the single mom to mix business and pleasure. But an undeniable attraction between Trish and Theo is distracting her from the task at hand....

ATHENA FORCE

Heart-pounding romance and thrilling adventure.

A ruthless enemy rises against the women of Athena Academy. In a global chess game of vengeance, kidnapping and murder, every move exposes potential enemies—and lovers. This time the women must stand together... before their world is ripped apart.

THIS NEW 12-BOOK SERIES BEGINS WITH A BANG IN AUGUST 2007 WITH

TRUST
by Rachel Caine

Look for a new Athena Force adventure each month wherever books are sold.

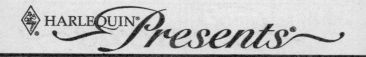

HARLEQUIN *Presents*

WIFE FOR
A WEEK
KELLY HUNTER

THE ELIGIBLE BACHELORS

They're strong, sexy, seductive..and single!

These gorgeous men are used to driving
women wild—they've got the looks, the cash
and that extra-special something....

They're also resolutely commitment-free! But
will these bachelors change their playboy
ways after meeting our four feisty females?

MISTRESS
ON TRIAL
KATE HARDY

MACALLISTER'S
BABY
JULIE COHEN

THE
FIREFIGHTER'S
CHOSEN BRIDE
TRISH WYLIE

Find out in August's collection from Promotional Presents!

WIFE FOR A WEEK by Kelly Hunter
MISTRESS ON TRIAL by Kate Hardy
MaCALLISTER'S BABY by Julie Cohen
THE FIREFIGHTER'S CHOSEN BRIDE by Trish Wylie

www.eHarlequin.com

HPP0807

BILLI✿NAIRES' BRIDES

Pregnant by their princes...

Take three incredibly wealthy European princes
and match them with three beautiful, spirited women.
Add large helpings of intense emotion and passionate
attraction. Result: three unexpected pregnancies...and
three possible princesses—if those princes have their way.

THE ITALIAN PRINCE'S
PREGNANT BRIDE
by Sandra Marton

It was payday for international tycoon Prince Nicolo Barbieri.
But he wasn't expecting what would come with his
latest acquisition: Aimee Black—who, it seemed,
was pregnant with Nicolo's baby!

Available in August.

Also available from this miniseries;

THE GREEK PRINCE'S CHOSEN WIFE
September

THE SPANISH PRINCE'S VIRGIN BRIDE
October